THE MEDUSA
FREQUENCY

RUSSELL HOBAN

THE MEDUSA FREQUENCY

THE ATLANTIC MONTHLY PRESS
NEW YORK

To Gundel

First published in Great Britain by Jonathan Cape Ltd, 1987
First Atlantic Monthly Press paperback edition, August 1990

Hoban, Russell.
  Medusa frequency / Russell Hoban.—1st ed.
  I. Title.
PS3558.0336M4   1987   813 '.54—dc19
ISBN 0-87113-165-X (hc)
      0-87113-368-7 (pb)

Printed in the United States of America

The Atlantic Monthly Press
19 Union Square West
New York, NY 10003

First printing

Contents

ZIP . . . POW . . . LOVES ME

George Herriman, 'Krazy Kat'

Same old story, same old song;
it goes all right till it goes all wrong.

Will Jennings, 'Same Old Story (Same Old Song)'

1 Art Is a Tough Business

I was shocked but I can't honestly say I was surprised when Istvan Fallok told me about Gösta Kraken. It could have been any one of us; art is a tough business.

I'm going to tell about what happened last November and early December. Whether it'll be of any use to anybody I don't know but I've been getting it all down on paper as it happened so here it is, beginning with the night when the flyer came through the letterbox.

2 First Appearance of the Kraken

NNVSNU TSRUNGH, said the green letters on the monitor screen of my Apple II computer that rainy night in November. This screen isn't like a piece of paper; the words come out of a green dancing and the excitation of phosphors. I'm the one who makes the words appear but I don't always know who or what is speaking.

Who's there? I said letter by letter on the screen.

No answer.

Speak up, I said. What are you afraid of?

NNVSNU TSRUNGH, it said.

You're afraid that you exist.

NNVSNU NNGH.

You don't want to exist.

NNVSNU RRNDU TS'IRNH TS'IRNH TS'IRNH NNGRH.

An existence such as yours is too dreadful to be thought of. Is this the Kraken speaking?

DON'T THINK OF ME. IF YOU THINK OF ME I MAY BE REAL. LET ME NOT BE REAL.

What was I to say to it? The reality of the Kraken isn't up to me, I'm not the final authority on such things. With its first words this creature was already as real to me as anything else; it was more real than the VAT figures that had appeared on this same screen the day before. The Customs and Excise Office isn't real to me in any way that really matters, it isn't there at three o'clock in the morning when the words come out of the green dancing and the singing comes from thousands of miles away.

No, what passes for reality seems to me mostly a load of old rubbish invented by not very inventive minds. The reality that interests me is strange and flickering and haunting. For example:

987 A SUPERB FIGURE OF A FISHERGIRL WITH A GIANT SQUID, the girl reclining with a contented expression as she

embraces the huge beast, whose skin is stippled, giving a mottled effect, its eyes inlaid in pearl with dark pupils, the group forming a long flat composition, the details are finely carved and the slightly worn ivory has a remarkable colour and patina, *early 19th century*. Ex F. Meinertzhagen collection. This is a magnificent Netsuke of a smooth compact form, ideal for its use.

There's a drawing of it in the book as well: the fishergirl entranced as with her left hand she grips the mantle of the squid whose eyes look up at her. She speaks to me, this fishergirl, and not simply as herself. Letter by letter words appear on the monitor screen:

Always in the dream are
the sea and the dream of the sea.
In the dream I am the fishergirl in
the twining embrace of the giant squid,
its dark eyes are on me as
it penetrates and inseminates me.

The giant squid has been dreaming of me age-long,
rising in the black night,
rising in the moony ocean night and never, never
    finding,
never until now finding
the mystery of me so long dreamt of, so long lusted
    after.
Eurydice, whispers the long sea, Eurydice, Eurydice,
and the giant squid is frightened by the beauty of me,
it trembles as it holds me in its twined embrace.

At three o'clock in the morning Eurydice is bound to come into it. After all, why did I sit here like a telegrapher at a lost outpost if not to receive messages from everywhere about the lost Eurydice who was never mine to begin with but whom I lamented and sought continually both professionally and amateurishly. This is not a digression. Where I am at three o'clock in the morning – and by now every hour is three o'clock in the morning – there are no digressions, it's all one thing.

LET ME NOT BE REAL, the Kraken said again.

There was nothing I could do about that and I didn't know what to say so I said nothing.

YOU DON'T TELL ME THAT I'M NOT REAL.

Again I didn't say anything.

THEN I AM REAL. I HAVE BEEN THOUGHT OF TOO MANY TIMES UNTIL THERE HAS COME TO BE SUCH A THING AS I, THE KRAKEN, LIVING WHERE I LIVE AND PERCIPIENT ALWAYS.

Tell me about your beginning.

IN THE BEGINNING OF ALL THINGS WAS MY BEGINNING, IN THE BEGINNING WAS THE TERROR.

Whose was the terror?

THE TERROR WAS ITSELF AND THE TERROR WAS OF ITSELF. THERE WAS NOTHING ELSE, THERE WAS NO ONE TO HOLD THE TERROR, THERE WAS ONLY THE TERROR.

Terror of what?

TERROR OF WHAT MIGHT BE, OF UNIVERSES AND WORLDS THAT MIGHT BE, AND THE ILLUSION OF TIME.

What came then?

FROM THE TERROR CAME THE AWARENESS OF IT. FROM THE TERROR CAME A TREMBLING AND A WRINKLING OF THE SILENCE THAT LISTENED.

Nothing else? No one to listen with the silence?

NO ONE TO LISTEN, NO ONE TO HOLD THE TERROR; ONLY THE ELECTRIC SILENCE THAT SHOOK AND WRINKLED AS IT BECAME YOUR MIND.

My mind holding the terror, my mind alone.

YOUR MIND HOLDING THE TERROR BUT IT WAS TOO MUCH FOR YOU TO HOLD ALONE. YOU THOUGHT OF ME AND YOU MADE ME HOLD THE TERROR THAT YOU COULD NOT HOLD. YOU THINK OF ME STILL, YOU THINK OF ME NOW.

I have always thought of you, have always had you in mind, have always heard the circles of your terror widening in the deeps. I think of you as the great cephalopod, ancient of the deeps, great thinking head in the blackness of the ultimate deep. I think of you as the Kraken. Even little children have an idea of you, they draw a great head with all the limbs growing out of it.

I AM THE KRAKEN, ANCIENT OF THE DEEPS, MONSTROUS CEPHALOPOD, GREAT HEAD AT THE CENTRE OF MY MILES OF WRITHING TENTACLES IN THE BLACKNESS OF THE ULTIMATE

DEEP; THE KRAKEN, MY DARK MIND WILD WITH THE TERROR OF ITSELF, SHUDDERING, WRITHING, AFRAID TO SLEEP, AFRAID TO DREAM BUT SLEEPING AGE-LONG AND DREAMING OF IMMENSITIES, OF BURSTINGS AND TRANSITIONS AND UNIMAGINABLE STATES OF BEING, DREAMING A UNIVERSE IN WHICH THERE IS SUCH A THING AS THE KRAKEN, DREAMING THAT I AM THE KRAKEN.

Will you show yourself to me?

I WILL SHOW MYSELF TO YOU IN SEVERAL WAYS AND WITH SEVERAL FACES.

Have you so many faces?

The Kraken said no more that night. But Eurydice has said in those three-o'clock-in-the-morning dancing green phosphors:

> Of me the terror, I squatted and gave birth:
> born of me the Kraken in its terror
> at the bottom of the sea. Born of me
> its terror of Eurydice.

3 The Vermeer Girl

My name is Herman Orff. At parties when people ask me what I do I say I'm a novelist and then they say, 'Oh, should I have heard of you?' and I say, 'I think not.' Then we both find somebody else to talk to.

My first novel, *Slope of Hell* (Mumchance Press, 1977), sold 1,731 copies before being remaindered. *The Times* found the writing 'a little slippery'; the *Guardian* noted that the story was 'a downhill sort of thing'. My second one, *World of Shadows* (Reedham & Weap, 1978), sold 1,247 copies before the publisher went into receivership. What I do for a living is write comics. I came to that via an advertising agency called Slithe & Tovey where I used to write copy for Orpheus Men's Toiletries, Hermes Foot Powder, Pluto Drain Magic, and several non-classical accounts. When we lost Hermes I was sacked and so was Sol Mazzaroth the account executive. Soon after that he became Editor in Chief of *Classic Comics* and that was the beginning of my freelance comic career. *Classic Comics* became for Sol Mazzaroth the earthen ramp by which he reached higher things, namely his own hardback imprint, the Avernus Press, where he published such rising talents as Boumboume Letunga, Hermione Thrust, and Juan de Fulmé. It was understood between us that my non-comic writing was not quite the thing for the Avernus list; I hewed wood and drew water at *Classic Comics* but I led my muse into insolvency elsewhere.

Working for *Classic Comics* wasn't too bad; it wasn't all that different from Slithe & Tovey: it was one of many bright and tastefully decorated places in London where people can neither speak nor write English and they say concept when they mean idea. The building was a posh little Bauhaus-style thing in High Holborn with a genuine Calder and a pseudo-Rothko in the waiting-room. Sol Mazzaroth had a big office full of layouts and proofs pinned up on corkboard and a lightbox littered with transparencies. It was better than Slithe & Tovey because I only had to be there when Sol wanted to talk to me about the work or when I delivered the finished adaptation of *Treasure Island* or *Ivanhoe* or whatever. After a few years of it I tended to see all speech in balloons and hear all sounds in expressionistic capital letters but that seemed a small price to pay for having the hours of my days under my own control.

Not having done terribly well with my first two novels I thought I might be third time lucky and I tried very hard to write another one but nothing came. Every afternoon I worked on my comics and every morning and night I tried to get a novel started. I could feel that there was life in my head, there were all sorts of things going on in it but nothing that could be made to act like a story for two or three hundred pages. Eight years had passed since I'd finished *World of Shadows* and so far page one of the next novel hadn't turned up. I thought of giving up writing but I didn't know how to do without that rush of panic and well-being that comes when I sit down at the word machine.

The night is my best time. At my lost outpost in Fulham I listen to my Drake R7 shortwave receiver while I work; it's a proper three-o-clock-in-the-morning radio, a black long-distance machine with two blue illuminated windows and a frequency counter with luminous red numbers. By now the two blue windows have gone dark and only the red numbers light up. As my thoughts appear letter by letter on the screen the voices come in from All India Radio or Radio Moscow or the Voice of Greece or Rias in Berlin or whoever's transmitting the music I crave at the time. I seldom listen to English broadcasts; I don't want to know what the words mean – I just want to hear those voices coming from far away in the night, coming round the curving ionosphere and the great globe-encircling miles, night miles, ocean miles where the deep fish glide in the deep, deep dark and the Kraken waits in the uttermost deep with its dark mind wild with the terror of itself and of Eurydice.

I tape a lot of the music that comes in; I seldom get a really clean recording of Bismillah Khan or Tatiana Petrova or whoever it might be but I like to hear the crackling, the twittering and tweetling and whispering, the sudden storms and surges of that particular transmission as it comes to me in

13

the night. Far, far away in the darkness are live human beings whose breathing can be heard as they speak and they're looking at their illuminated dials as I look at mine at this end of the thousands of great globe-encircling miles, ocean miles in the night, the heave and swell and the deep fish gliding in the dark. And always on the night air sweet women singing in all the tongues of humankind, singing to the accompaniment of strange instruments, strange rhythms in places unseen but existing at this very moment, perhaps with red dust rising on the plains or monsoon rains beating down or snow on mountain peaks impassable. And while I hear those sweet voices singing words that I cannot understand I watch my thoughts appear letter by letter in the green dancing of the phosphors on the monitor screen.

My desk is a clutter of stones written upon and not; seashells, acorns and oak leaves, china mermaids from long-gone aquaria, postcards of medieval carven lions, clockwork frogs and photographs of distant moments. It's a good desk, there's a lot of action even when I'm not there. Propped up amongst the stones and clutter are two books open at colour plates of Vermeer's *Head of a Young Girl*; there are also a postcard of it stuck on the edge of the monitor screen and a large print over the fireplace. Night and day in all weathers she looks out at me from her hereness and her goneness. Even the ageing of the painting seems organic to it; one can see in the reproductions how the reticulation of fine cracks in the paint follows lovingly from light into shadow the curve of her cheek, the softness of her mouth, the glisten of her eyes, the fineness of brow and nose, the delicacy of her chin.

Impossible to know what her look might have been a response to; presumably Vermeer sat down at the easel and said something like, 'Turn your body to the side but turn your face to me. No, back a little – like that. Hold it like that.' And she'd held it like that, her face full of questioning and uncertainty. Was there also fear? Fear of what? What had she to fear from him? Was the giant squid in her thoughts or in her dreams? What was her name? Maybe it will come to me, the story of what happened between them. Here it comes, no research – straight story:

14

Vermeer when he painted this picture was forty-five. He'd been married for a quarter of a century and had seven children when there sat down in front of him this girl of seventeen. Her name was Ursula; they called her Ursel, Oor-zl. When you say her name it isn't like saying Miranda for example; it's a simpler utterance.

Ursel, he used to say in his mind as she went her ways about the house. She was a servant; he paid her money and she lived in his house, slept under his roof. He imagined her lying in the darkness at the top of the house; he imagined the smell of her warmth and the sound of her breathing in the darkness.

When he said, 'Will you sit for me, Ursel?' she said, 'Yes, Mynheer.' There was no question of getting her to take her clothes off, he wanted her nakedness so much that he couldn't ask for it, he had to put more clothes on her. 'Try this,' he said, handing her the blue and gold scarf. He stood watching as she wound it round her head. 'Yes,' he said, hearing the sound of her breathing in the darkness, 'that's good. Now turn and look at me the way you did before. Like that. Hold it like that.'

She sat that day and the next and the next while he painted. Looked at her and painted. The look on her face is her answer to his look. That was all that happened.

After writing the above I looked at the back of the postcard of the painting and noted that Vermeer only lived to be forty-three.

I went down to the kitchen and made myself a sardine sandwich. While I ate it I leafed through *Personal Computer World* looking at the various ads for hardware and software. There were so many software packages for spreadsheets and databases and computer adventure games, why couldn't there be one called *Third Novel*?

On my way back to my desk I noticed something lying on the floor by the front door where I always find cards and notices from radio cars and estate agents, carpet cleaners, palmists, and Chinese takeaways. This one was typed on yellow paper, the same kind I use:

ART TROUBLE?
COMPOSERS, WRITERS, FILM-MAKERS —
STUCK? NOTHING HAPPENING? NO IDEAS?
WHY NOT
HEAD FOR IT?

Write orph one
HERMES

Write orph one? There were a Soho address and telephone number. I sat down at my desk, put a stone from Paxos on the HERMES flyer, and looked at the Vermeer girl in the postcard, the two books, and the print over the fireplace. The look on her face always made me think of Luise von Himmelbett who lived with me for two years and left me nine years ago. There's a photograph of an olive tree among the stones on my desk; when Luise left she wrote on the back of it:

I trusted you with the idea of me
and you lost it.

4 Hermes Soundways

Later that Monday when I'd had some sleep and the day was open for business I looked out of the window and saw that it was grey and glistening and rainy. Good, I thought; more things happen when it's grey and glistening and rainy.

When I rang the HERMES number a breathy female voice, shadowy and warm, said, 'Hermes Soundways'. In the background there was music, veiled and flickering but familiar.

'Hermes *Soundways*,' I said as I remembered. Hermes Soundways was Istvan Fallok, he'd been Luise von Himmelbett's lover before me. Back then Luise was working at the Netherworld Bookshop in Kensington Church Street around the corner from Slithe & Tovey; I went in there for a classical dictionary and that was the first time I saw her.

She was twenty-seven then, taller than I, with the sort of old-fashioned beauty one sees in antique dolls; she had a long shining plait of blonde hair, a lovely voice, a very short skirt, and wonderful legs. She sold me *The Oxford Classical Dictionary* as well as eight other books of which the last was *Giordano Bruno and the Hermetic Tradition*; I still haven't read it and I don't ever expect to but I'd have bought whatever she showed me. When I told her I was going to be writing copy for Orpheus and Hermes she said that she knew a composer who was obsessed with those particular themes and that's how I came to meet Istvan Fallok.

It wasn't at all surprising that I should fall in love with Luise; I'd been divorced not long before that, I was alone, and I'd never met a woman like her: she was quite calm just being herself, she had none of the desperation that produces art, she commanded attention without producing a product. I asked her to lunch and she said yes. I took her to Mr Chow in Knightsbridge. I haven't been there for years now but that was back when I bathed and shaved every morning and sometimes did that sort of thing at lunchtime. I asked if Fallok was a special friend of hers and she told me they'd been together for

17

two years but it was over now. 'I kept my bedsit in Kilburn the whole time,' she said, 'I never moved in with him.'

'You knew it wasn't going to last?'

'One woman's not enough for Istvan,' she said.

'I can't imagine being with you and wanting anyone else,' I said.

'Why is that?'

'Because you're everything I've ever wanted in a woman.'

'Are you sure? I'm not clever, you know – I don't write or paint or anything like that, I'm not an intellectual type.'

'An intellectual type isn't what I'm after.'

'What are you after then?'

'You,' I said. 'You're what I'm after.' The world at that moment was so various, so beautiful, so new, the very air was electric with good luck and happy promise, I could feel her responding to the excitement in me. I was thirty-eight then; I was in a heightened state of mating behaviour, able to catch the waiter's eye, to find taxis or parking spaces without frustration, to get interval drinks at the theatre without groaning, to buy tickets for concerts and recitals – nothing was burdensome to me, nothing was too much trouble, and she was the woman who would make everything all right. I imagined waking up and finding her there every morning, I imagined page after page coming out of the typewriter. I wrote poems, gave presents, wooed early and late, and within two months she'd left her Kilburn bedsit and was living with me.

'Are you there?' said the shadowy female voice on the telephone.

'I'm ringing about a flyer I got through my letterbox,' I said.

'Hang on,' she said.

'Hello,' said a man's voice.

'Is that Istvan Fallok?'

'Yes. Who's this?'

'Herman Orff.'

'Ah, art trouble. Stuck, are we?'

'It happens. I seem to remember that it's even happened to you on occasion.'

'Lots of occasions. Funny, I've got that Hermes theme on the Revox now, you can probably hear it. Seen Luise lately?'

18

'No, it's been more than nine years. Have you?'

'No. Our lost Eurydice.'

'Are you still composing electronic music?'

'Sure. I did the track for *Codename Orpheus*. Have you seen it?'

'No. Is it a spy film?'

'More of an existential exploration of the nature of reality.'

'Listen, what's this HEAD FOR IT thing?'

'It's an EEG technique with a few refinements.'

'Will it get me to places in my head that I haven't been able to get to?'

'Maybe you've already been to all the places there are in your head.'

'I'll take that chance. Has it got you anywhere you hadn't got to before?'

'Yes, it has. But it mightn't be a place you want to get to.'

'How much are you charging for it?'

'Fifty quid for the first hour, twenty-five for every hour after that.'

'How soon can we do it?'

'Can you come between three and four this afternoon?'

'Yes.'

'Right. See you then.'

'See you.'

Strange, talking to Fallok after all those years. I wondered if he still had any hard feelings about me and Luise. He'd said at the time that he'd known she was going to leave him sooner or later. She was a loyal woman but very proud.

The Vermeer girl was looking at me from the two books, the postcard, and the print over the fireplace. I had no idea where Luise was now.

In the afternoon I left for Soho. Fulham Broadway is one of those underground stations that look like aeroplane hangars, airy and light and full of lift and more so on a rainy day. People made their entrances and took their places on the platform, each of them more or less in character for the day's performance. I was playing Herman Orff in *The Quest*.

There was a leggy young woman in a short black skirt, black leather jacket, black tights, and little black boots, clip-clop, clip-clop. She turned as she passed, her eyes seemed wide with surprise. Her hair was brown and thick – she was altogether urban but she looked as if she might vanish behind a tree. Her eyes were remarkable: dark eyes darkly outlined, open wide so that when she looked at me there was white all round the pupil. Her eyes were not like the eyes of women on Greek vases but there came the thought of a shady grove. The grove became more shadowy, became wild woodland. Her face had a sudden woodland look, as if she might just that moment have heard the baying of hounds.

Don't be ridiculous, I said to myself as I drifted along to where she was. She was leaning against a pillar reading a book; it was a proof copy. With some casual twisting and bending I was able to make out the title: *The Mountains of Orgasma* by Juan de Fulmé, published by Avernus. Juan de Fulmé had won last year's Booker Prize with *The Valley of Pudenda*. O God! I thought: to explore the valley of her pudenda! To climb with her the mountains of Orgasma! Don't be ridiculous, I told myself again but it was no use whatever.

I reminded myself that I was forty-nine and wondered how old this woman of the wood might be: about twenty-seven, I thought. Beauty that passes! Transience! Was I going to be foolish? It looked as if I was. I didn't want to be old and wise, wisdom seemed unsporting; I wanted to be more foolish than when I was young, I'd never been foolish enough. What is it but foolishness that brings the giant squid and Eurydice together? Non-giants also are subject to it.

From far off in the blackness came a moving light, the wincing of the rails ran towards us ahead of the rumble and clatter of the train. Doors opened before us, closed behind us, we swayed and shook as one in *Transports of Darkness* by Herman Orff; *Caverns of Iron* by Herman Orff; *Upward the Light*, a trilogy? NOTTING HILL GATE, said the sign outside the window. Doors opened, we got out. Ahead of me with forms of walking world between us she clip-clopped through that buskerless corridor to the Central Line escalators. No pipes, no timbrels; only the pattering clock of footsteps measuring multitudes of separate mortalities.

Her quiet reading face replayed itself in my mind as her legs beckoned before me, descending to the platform where we stood and looked into the tunnel for a light. ORPHEUS TRAVEL, said a poster in pseudo-Greek lettering. I will, I answered in pseudo-Greek.

Again we shook together, swayed together, were entranced together in our space of light that rumbled through the darkness. We both got off at Oxford Circus. On Argyll Street I saw her before me, umbrellaless and vivid in the greyness and the rain. What a pleasure it must be for her to walk around in her body, I thought as I watched the glisten of the street flashing at her swift dark heels. She crossed Great Marlborough Street, went into Carnaby and over to Marshall which was the way I was legitimately going: Hermes Soundways was off Broadwick Street round the corner from Cranks Wholefood Restaurant. The rain intensified the colours of the present and called up the past that always waits, the colours of it unremembered, the light of it strange on my eyes. Luise and I used to drink rose-hip tea at Cranks.

This new woman of the rainy afternoon continued ahead of me to the alley where Hermes Soundways was. Very Soho, the little alley of Istvan Fallok. Full of little businesses looked in upon by dusty windows. Little hidden businesses in the rain, in the greyness, ledgers and invoices unknown, services unrecognized. There were many gaunt and angular scaffoldings suggestive of Piranesi's prison fantasies, dark against the grey sky. Dark pipes and planking in the rainlight of Soho, in the greylight of Istvan Fallok's little corner of the world where she was obviously going.

A flight of steps led down to his place, through the windows I could see a shadowy interior glowing with illuminated dials and little eyes of red and green and yellow light; she clip-clopped down the steps ahead of me without looking round. When he opened the door I heard, veiled and flickering, the same music I'd heard on the telephone; this place lived in the half-light of its music and in the music of its half-light, it swam in sound like a long-drowned city in a sea of dreams.

Here sleeps the Kraken, I thought:

> Unnumber'd and enormous polypi
> Winnow with giant arms the slumbering green.

The music was part of the look of the place and of Istvan Fallok; the music and the half-light clung to him like the smell of the roll-ups that he used to smoke continually when he and I were working on Hermes. He didn't look like his name, didn't look dark and eastern. He was forty-three, tall and thin, with lank red hair and a long white face and pale hard blue eyes with dark circles under them and he looked awful. He'd never been a very robust or healthy type but now he looked haunted. He was twisting a piece of red insulated wire in his hands. Maybe he's just stopped smoking, I thought, nothing more than that. 'Hi,' he said and kissed the young woman, then he saw me and said 'Hi' again and we shook hands.

'Nice to see you again,' I said.

'It's been a while. You two know each other?'

She turned around, looked at me and smiled. 'No.' I SAW YOU STARING AT ME, said her eyes.

YOU KNOW WHAT I WANT, said my eyes.

'Melanie Falsepercy; Herman Orff,' said Fallok.

'Hello,' she said. For a moment her hand lay in mine. IT'S POSSIBLE, said her hand. Her face looked intently at my face. 'You don't look like your jacket photo.'

'Time passes,' I said.

'I've read your books,' she said. Her voice was the one that had answered Fallok's telephone, breathy and shadowy and there was something heartbreaking in it: youth with the world before it; youth and the world passing, passing; stay yet awhile! She'll be alive when I'm dead, I thought, but never mind, it's a sporting proposition, go in to win. Was I in shape for it? Film stars ten years older than I ran lightly up the stairs but I'd found it hard to keep up with her walking from Oxford Circus to Fallok's place. Was I going to need a rope for the Mountains of Orgasma? What about the Cliffs of Angina? Wouldn't it have been simpler just to be born twenty years later? On the other hand, when I was twenty-nine I hadn't yet written the books that had aroused her interest. Could I have been interesting at twenty-nine without the books?

'I read *World of Shadows* three times,' she said.

'Thank you,' I said. 'I knew this was going to be a good day.'

'I can't stay,' she said to Fallok, 'I only wanted to drop off the tape.' She gave him a cassette. I wondered what was on the tape, I wondered what was between them. 'See you,' she said to him. 'Nice meeting you,' she said to me, and her legs took her up the steps and away into the rain.

I LOVE YOU, I transmitted with my mind. I PROMISE TO BE FOOLISH.

YOU'LL BE SORRY, said her departing legs.

'The place looks about the same,' I said to Fallok as we went into the studio. 'A little more technological maybe.'

'Did her legs say something to you just now?' he said.

'I wasn't really listening.'

'That'll be the day.'

'Strange name, Falsepercy. Is it from the French: *Faux-percé*, the false pierced?'

'I don't know. I don't speak French.'

'What does she do?'

'She's a reader at the Avernus Press.'

'What a small world it is.'

'And crowded,' he said.

All around in the dusk of the room watched and waited the little eyes of coloured light. An Anglepoise lamp on a drawing table in a corner made an island of bright warmth. Pinned up among notes, announcements, posters and photographs on an expanse of corkboard was a large print of *Head of a Young Girl*. There was a Melanie Falsepercy look in her eyes.

On a table near the door was something that looked like a piano keyboard. On top of its housing sat a computer keyboard; to the right of it was a visual display unit from which hung a lightpen. Under the table was a box for the computer works and the double disk drive. On the screen in luminous green letters was a double row of names beginning with ORPHEUS and EURYDICE.

'Is that a music computer?' I said.

'Yes, it's a Fairlight.'

'And ORPHEUS and EURYDICE are voices you've got loaded into it?'

'That's right.'

'Is Luise the Eurydice voice?'

'Yes. Anything else you need to know?'

'Is that still the Hermes music I'm hearing?'

'Yes.'

'There's really no foot powder at all in it, is there?'

23

'That's what the client said at the presentation. Shall we get started?'

'How does it work?'

'I've got it set up over here.' He indicated several circuit boards thick with condensers, transistors, resistors, silicon chips and vari-coloured wiring. On each was a fascia with authentic-looking gauges and dials; connected to one of them were leads to a harness obviously meant for the subject's head; there were also a scientific sort of printer and a revolving drum with a pen for recording the brain waves. The whole thing looked reassuringly ordinary; I might possibly be electrocuted but other than that it seemed safe enough.

'I use thirty-six electrodes to build up a reference grid,' he said. 'When you're hooked up I'll ask you to say a couple of words about what you're after. From that this receiver will give me a digital printout of signal strength and frequencies from each of the thirty-six electrodes. With those data I can work out a complementary sonic pattern on the Fairlight and I'll feed that into the headphones you'll be wearing. When I get both patterns in sync I'll send a low-powered charge to selected electrodes. It's just a little more juice than your brain generates and it excites the neurons in such a way that it might or might not get you to those places in your head that you can't get to on your own.'

'It did it for you, right?'

'Oh yes, it did it for me.'

'How many times have you done it?'

'Just once.'

'Just once. And that was . . .'

'All I needed.'

'Did it help with your music?'

'Hard to say.'

'But at least it didn't do any harm?'

'Do I look as if it's done me any harm?'

'I don't know,' I said. He looked as if *something* had done him harm, but then so did I, I supposed.

'Well,' he said, 'shall we do it?'

I'd better not, I thought. 'Yes,' I said. 'Let's do it.' He was still twisting the piece of wire. 'Where's your Golden Virginia?' I said. 'Why aren't you smoking?'

24

'I stopped.' He dabbed electrolytic cream on the thirty-six locations and with great precision harnessed up my head with the thirty-six electrodes and put the headphones on me. Then he switched on the frequency counter and the computer-printer. Various new red and green and yellow lights winked on, adding to the watchfulness of the already attentive room.

'OK,' he said, 'we're operational; is there a particular place in your head you're trying to get to?'

I'd been listening to the Hermes music that had become a field charged with energies not of this moment. My mouth opened and I heard it say, 'The olive tree.' I hadn't intended to say that.

'Right, the olive tree. Can you say a little more about it? I want to see what kind of a reading we get.'

In the Hermes music the particles of time past coalesced into sunlight on the island of Paxos, the summer air warm on my face, and Luise and I walking to the beach. It was our second summer and our last. The road that led from the hills down into the town passed between terraces of olive groves dry-walled with grey and white stones. There were empty blue plastic mineral-water bottles everywhere, there were thrown-away cookers and meat-grinders rusting in the olive groves. The trees had been planted long, long ago before there were such things as plastic mineral-water bottles; for hundreds of years they had twisted their roots into the stony earth of their stone-walled terraces. The tree that I was thinking of was one that we always stopped to look at. Often there was a black donkey tethered to it, sometimes there was a black-and-white goat nearby. When the donkey opened wide its jaws and brayed it made the most tremendous heehaw, it was like the creaking of the door of the world. It was much too big a sound for a donkey to make, it was as if something else was making itself heard through the donkey. When the goat was there it looked calmly at us with its strange eyes that were like tawny grey stones in which were set oblongs of black stone. Most of the time there was a cock crowing somewhere amongst the mineral-water bottles. The tree was alive, the sunlight sang and twittered in the silvery leaves and the olives made black dots against the sky. Yet the trunk was empty, it was only the shell of a tree with darkness inside the ancient lithe and ardent shape

25

of it. The greenish-grey thick bark all ridged and wrinkled stood open as if two hands had parted it, as if a woman or a goddess had stepped naked out of it into the greenlit shade of the olive grove.

Luise and I had often talked about this tree; we agreed that it was an entrance to the underworld, a Persephone door. Now on this particular morning she went to the tree and stood before it with her hands on the two sides of the opening. The skirt of her little white beach dress stirred in the warm air; the August sunlight was elegiac through the whispering leaves.

'Are you talking to Persephone?' I said.

'Yes. She's been telling me about the underworld; it isn't what people think it is, it isn't just a place for the dead. What we call world is only that little bit of each moment that we know about – underworld is everything else that we don't know but we need it. Underworld is like the good darkness where the olive tree has its roots. Did you know that?'

'I suppose I did.'

'But what if it's a bad darkness? What if it's a darkness in which people tell lies and are deceitful? How does one live then, Herman?'

'What are you getting at?' But I knew.

'You know very well what I'm getting at. I was looking in your writing folder for stamps and I found a letter.'

'*Can* you say something about the olive tree?' said Fallok.

'Persephone lives in it,' I said.

Paper came out of the printer in perfect silence like a mystic arm from the water. Fallok studied it.

'Have you got your reading?' I said.

'Yes, I've got it.' He was busy with the Fairlight while the Hermes that was not foot powder danced in the electronic twilight not as a picture in the mind but as a mode of event, a shift in the relativities of the moment, a new disposition of probabilities. The music that drifted through the dusk and the little coloured lights seemed a way through the olive grove to the tree that stood open as if a naked woman or a goddess had parted the wrinkled greenish-grey bark with her hands and stepped out into the greenlit shade.

I turned to the Vermeer girl on the corkboard. The look on her face was a look that made no attempt to avert anything. The music in my headphones, while still moving forward, seemed never to depart; other shapes configured themselves to it in a moire that shimmered in my head like a watered silk of sound.

'OK,' said Fallok. 'Here it comes.' He pushed a button. The dusk poured itself into darkness, the darkness inside the tree, the dark entrance. I saw into the darkness, saw down into the earth where all around me, as if the dark were silvered like a mirror, I saw a face, a face not mine, a face not clear but almost recognizable, with a speaking mouth saying words almost intelligible.

'Persephone?' I said, dropping, dropping, faster and faster through the darkness, down, down into the blackness at the bottom of the sea. The blackness thickened crushingly, became millstones of blackness grinding my brain. The eyes of the Vermeer girl, of Luise, of Melanie Falsepercy dilated enormously and disappeared into the vast pulpy head that shuddered for ever in the chill of the ultimate deep.

Blackness, blackness, black water pressing down on me for ever, all the sunlight, all the daylight gone for ever into ancient night. The tentacles convulsed in vast and writhing tremors; widening in clangorous circles came the waves of terror spreading from the brute bell of the first great terror of Creation. Ah, that the possible should burst out of the blackness! That there should be no rest, no ease, no comfort! That there should be life and world and that all, all, should return to the blackness, even the sun itself gone cold and dead and shrunken back to blackness. Drowning, I gasped and shuddered in the moment that would not depart, ascending through black, blue-black, deep blue, blue-green, deep green, sunlit green. With me rose the great head of the Kraken, terror in its eyes. We broke the surface, there was sunlight hot on my face, dancing in a million sunpoints on the rocking ocean, dazzling in my eyes.

Rolling in the rocking sea, green-slimed and barnacled, the great head filled my vision. It was a human head, rotting and eyeless. It was enormous, a floating island over which seabirds wheeled crying under the heartless blue of the sky. I tried to climb on to it as it rolled but my fingers slipped on the green slime and I scraped my flesh bloody on the barnacles as I fell back into the water. The great cavern of the mouth opened and showed its white teeth, its red tongue, its cry was like the rending of mountains. 'Eurydice!' it bellowed, 'Eurydice!' as the seabirds rose up screaming.

I clung to the hair that floated round the head and undulated with the swell. Looking down into the water I saw rising a vast and ivory nakedness and a woman's face of terrifying beauty. Her red-gold hair streamed round her, her green eyes were open wide, her pale silent mouth was open.

Closer and closer came the face of Eurydice, her mouth open and grinning, her tongue hanging out. Larger and larger grew her face, widening in my vision until I saw it all around me, this great and loosely grinning face of the Vermeer girl and Melanie Falsepercy and Luise becoming, becoming . . . Who were they becoming?

'Luise,' I said, 'Luise, Luise.'

'I used to know a Louisa,' said the man on my right as the sunlit sea slid past the window. LANCASTER GATE appeared and was gone. He had an unsure look and was wearing a broken-brimmed hat.

'How do you spell it?' I said.

He pulled up his jacket sleeve and his shirt sleeve and showed me a tattoo on his forearm, a snake twined around a dagger. On a little banner above it was the name *Louisa*. 'Like that,' he said.

'Not the same,' I said. 'Why the snake and the dagger?'

'Symbolic.'

'Of what?'

'I don't know, I was drunk when I had it done.'

'Where's Louisa now?'

'No idea, no idea at all. Snows of yesteryear. She may have become a lion-tamer, she may have joined the Navy. You break out of the bin?'

'Why? Do I look like a loony?'

'Look like you been plugged into the wall or something.'

It was then that I became aware of the wires trailing from the electrodes on my head. I unwired myself and was going to put everything into the pocket of my anorak but I wasn't wearing my anorak and now that I noticed it I was cold. I stuffed the wires and the electrodes into a trouser pocket.

'You been getting some kind of ECT,' he said. 'They done that to me, they said the voices would go away.'

'Did they?'

'Yes. Now I've got nothing. There's only a kind of ringing emptiness. I never asked them to take away the voices but there it is, you see: who am I? Nobody. I'm not entitled to hear voices unless it's somebody asking me questions and taking down what I say. You showed them though, you just walked away wires and all. Don't let them empty you out, they've got nothing better to offer. Best of luck to you is what I say.' He shook my hand warmly and gave me a thumbs-up sign when I got off at Notting Hill Gate.

When I was alone the sea came back to me again, I could feel the running of the tide as I went up the escalators, through the corridor and up the stairs to the District and Circle Line platforms. Everything seemed much dårker than it ought to be. I went to the end of the platform where I always wait for the Wimbledon train and stood looking at a narrow vertical sign that said A162, a light that showed sometimes red and sometimes green, and a distorting mirror. In the mirror the tracks rippled as if straightness were not the truth of the black tunnels. The unseen olive tree and the sea flickered their sunlight in the November dark.

A bright stillness approached, on the front of it the illuminated word WIMBLEDON. Listening to the sea I entered it, was borne home through November dark and moving lights, poured myself a large gin, was very tired, took the phone off the hook, fell asleep on the couch.

It was between six and seven in the morning. The moon was low in the sky. It was a waxing moon, a gibbous one; it was a particular moon. I raised the window-blind. The pinky-orange hibiscus street lamp outside the window was the same as always. I opened the front door and went out into the fore-dawn, into the hissing of the silence and the humming of the underground trains standing empty with lighted windows on the far side of the common. Unseen birds twittered but there was no crow to shout and flaunt its blackness.

I heard my footsteps; I saw under the lamps my shadow first before me, then behind. 'Nothing to declare,' I said.

I crossed the common and headed down the New King's Road. The Belisha beacons clicked as they blinked in the

29

coldness of the morning. Cars at intervals hissed past me, in each one a face as questionable as the faces printed on the tin windows of toy cars from Japan. The shops stood like sleeping horses.

The lamps on Putney Bridge were still lit, the bridge stood in simple astonishment over the water, a stonelike creature of overness, of parapets and ghostly pale cool tones of blue, of grey, of dim whiteness in the foredawn with its lamps lit against a sky growing light. Far below lay the river; slack-water it was, turn of the tide, the low-tide river narrow between expanses of mud, the moored boats rocking on the stillness.

A sort of singing filled my head; it seemed an aspect of the particles of light and colour that made in my eyes the picture of this time just before dawn. I thought of the dew on the grass where the olive tree stood. There seemed to be a question in the air.

'Yes,' I said, 'I will.' I spoke aloud because I wanted my answer to be recorded on the early air.

I was walking on the Putney side of the river, walking on the low-tide beach, hearing the lapping of the water on the stones. I was seeing the moon-glints on the water, I was smelling the low-tide smell of the mud and the stones by the river.

The singing in my head became the slowly spreading circles of an intolerable clangour; it was as if the brute bell of the universe were caged in my mind and bursting my skull. 'Eurydice!' whispered a voice from the mud, from the stones. 'Eurydice!'

5 The Head of Orpheus Begins Its Story

It was an eyeless and bloated human head, sodden, covered with green slime and heavy with barnacles. I took it in my hands; where the flesh had been eaten away I could feel the ancient skull.

I could feel the head humming and buzzing in my hands, then it began to speak. Its voice was more elemental, more profound than human voices are; the way it spoke seemed more animal than human; it was as if speech had suddenly become possible for an animal, as if the creature were for the first time putting thoughts into words. 'Who are you?' said the head.

'Nobody, really. Nobody you'd know.'

'You wouldn't be seeing me if I didn't know you. What's your name?'

I didn't want to tell it my name.

'Speak up,' said the head. 'What are you afraid of?'

'Everything.'

'No you aren't, you came to the river and you said, "Yes, I will."'

'I don't know why I said that.'

'Tell me your name.'

'Herman Orff.'

'Is that really your name?'

'Yes, it really is.'

'Do you know who I am?'

'No. Who are you?'

'I'm the head of Orpheus.'

'How do you do.'

'You sound as if you don't believe me.'

'Why aren't you speaking Greek?'

'The words that I'm speaking are what I find in your mind. Is there any Greek there?'

'No.'

'That's why I'm not speaking Greek.'

'Oh yes.'

'You still don't believe me. Do you want me to sing for you?'

'All right, sing for me.'

The head opened its mouth, its lips and tongue moved, I felt it vibrate in my hands but I heard nothing. After a long time the vibration stopped. 'Well?' said the head.

'I didn't hear anything.'

The head began to weep, it shook in my hands with great wild racking sobs. After a while it quieted down.

'Look,' I said, 'it's all right, I believe you without the singing.'

'You don't believe me the way I want you to believe me, I can hear it in your voice – you don't believe I'm the real head of Orpheus.'

'In the first place I do believe you, and in the second place how much difference does it make if you aren't the real head of Orpheus? I'm not sure I'm the real head of Herman Orff but I get up every morning and get on with it. You're what you are and I'm what I am and let's leave it at that.'

'All right, you believe that I'm the head of Orpheus. But do you believe that I'm real?'

'Real how?'

'Like the river, like the stones and the mud.'

'I believe you're real in your way.'

'What way is that?'

'You're real in my mind; you're a hallucination.'

'Do you think I'll go away if you stop thinking me?'

'Yes, I do.'

'And what if I stop thinking you?'

'I think I'll still be here.'

'Let's try it,' said the head, and was gone; in my hands I held a slime-covered stone. There was a greyness all around me, a tightness across my chest, a heaviness coming to a point on each side of the base of my throat, the veins and arteries of my arms seemed filled with lead. The pain grew harder and heavier; I thought I was going to collapse there in the mud by the river. Then the head was back in my hands, the greyness and the pain receded.

'That's what happens if I stop thinking you,' said the head of Orpheus. 'Do you know what I am to you?'

32

'Probably not.'

'I am the first of your line. I am the first singer, the one who invented the lyre, the one to whom Hermes brought Eurydice and perpetual guilt. I am your progenitor, I am the endlessly voyaging sorrow that is always in you, I am that astonishment from which you write in those brief moments when you can write.'

'Endlessly voyaging sorrow and astonishment. Yes, I have those from you, I know that. Perpetual guilt, you said.'

'In the stories they always say I turned around to look at her too soon but that isn't how it was: I turned *away* too soon, turned away before I'd ever looked long enough, before I'd ever fully perceived her.'

With those words there came into my mind Luise. Once when we were living together I was on a 22 bus and I saw her unexpectedly in Sloane Street. The bus was moving slowly north in heavy traffic and she was walking south. She was wearing a long black coat and as she approached she was smiling to herself and walking slowly, lingeringly, as if lost in thought. Then the bus passed her and I turned and saw her going away. After that I sometimes imagined her seen from a distance walking away slowly, lingeringly, not coming back.

'Does anyone ever fully perceive anyone else?' I said. I began to cry.

'Cry on my face,' said the head, 'maybe my eyes will grow back.'

'Is there healing in my tears?'

'I don't know, I'll try anything.'

'Maybe you ought to stop trying. You're old, you're blind and rotten, you can't sing any more. Why don't you just pack it in?'

'I haven't that choice, there's no way for me to cease to be. I'm manifesting myself to you as a rotting head but there's no picture for what I am: I am that which sings the world, I am the response that never dies. Fidelity is what's wanted.'

'Fidelity. I got my head zapped looking for a novel and here I am listening to homilies from a rotting head.'

'You don't know what you're looking for,' said the head. 'Alone and blind and endlessly voyaging I think constantly of fidelity. Fidelity is a matter of perception; nobody is unfaithful to the sea or to mountains or to death: once recognized they fill the heart. In love or in terror or in loathing one responds to them with the true self; fidelity is not an act of the will: the soul is compelled by recognitions. Anyone who loves, anyone who perceives the other person fully can only be faithful, can never be unfaithful to the sea and the mountains and the death in that person, so pitiful and heroic is it to be a human being.'

Again I felt the pain across my chest and down my left arm. 'If you're going to take a high moral tone you'd better find someone else to talk to,' I said, 'I'm not up to it.'

'Do you think about fidelity sometimes?' said the head.

'Sometimes.' Years after Luise had gone I found inside a copy of Rilke's *Neue Gedichte* her recipe for bread; I'd never seen her use a written-down recipe but there it was in her writing on a folded-up feint-ruled notebook page marking 'Orpheus, Eurydike, Hermes':

1·5 kg granary flour
2 dessertsp oil
1   "   salt
1 tblesp caraway seeds
2   "   dried yeast
1½ pts water, bloodwarm
1 teasp sugar

Put flour in a bowl, add oil & caraway seeds. Put sugar & yeast in a jug, add a little of the warm water. Leave for 10–15 mins in a warm place to froth, add salt to warm water. When yeast dissolved, add to the flour and water. Stir, then turn on to a floured board & knead 10–15 mins until it is elastic. Put back in bowl, cover, leave to rise in warm place. When doubled in size, take out, divide into 2, knead & thump, shape into loaves and put in greased tins. Cover, leave for 10 mins in a warm place, then put in oven & bake at 220° for 40–5 mins.

The smell of the brown loaves was like fidelity.

Luise had an accordion and she liked to play hymns on it. Her favourite was 'Aus Tiefer Not', 'From Deep Distress':

> *Aus tiefer Not schrei ich zu dir,*
> *Herr Gott, erhör mein Rufen.*

> From deep distress cry I to thee,
> Lord God, hear thou my calling.

This is Psalm 130, 'De profundis', and the *Book of Common Prayer* renders it:

> Out of the deep have I called unto thee, O Lord:
> Lord, hear my voice.

She sang it in German of course, in a deep and distant Thirty Years' War soprano while the accordion marched on in a minor key like a troop of pikemen with dinted helmets. Luise's mother had bought her the accordion and paid for the lessons; her father had died in the Ardennes in 1944.

She farted like a woman who carries a spear and drives a chariot. 'What kind of piety is that?' I said. 'With your upper part you're singing hymns and with your lower part you're making *Götterdämmerung*. You're making *tiefe Not* for the rest of the world.'

'They can cry out to God the same as I do. The airwaves are free, it costs them nothing.'

'Tell me more about your deep distress.'

'With you everything comes out; with me it stays in, it's deep, it's nothing to talk about. Also it's not uncomfortable, it's like a mountain of stone and on top of it grows a little blue flower. Don't worry about it.'

'The mountain stays in but the bad air comes out.'

'Inside I'm pure,' she said.

'Is there something else you wanted to talk about?' I said to the head. 'Or is fidelity the only thing on your mind at the moment?'

'Do you want to hear my story?' said the head.

'Yes, I want to hear your story.'

'I ask you for the second time: do you want to hear my story?'

'Yes, please tell it.'

'I'll ask you three times: for the third time, do you want to hear my story?'

'Yes, yes, yes. Three times yes. Now tell it.'

'Once begun, the story must be finished.'

'Well of course I want to hear the whole thing.'

35

'You have to take it on you then, you have to say, "Once begun, the story must be finished; I take it on me."'

'Once begun, the story must be finished; I take it on me.'

'Now I'll begin,' said the head. 'I'm not very sure of anything; I may be lying or I may even be making it up as I go along. I was a good musician but I'm not reliable in any other way. Sometimes I can't make the distinction between how things seemed and how they actually were.'

'Who can?'

The head of Orpheus gave a little cough and seemed to pull itself together. 'I don't really want to tell my story,' it said, 'but I have to do it if I ask three times and you say yes each time. I'm not even sure what the story is. Have you ever, perhaps while walking, found the world coming towards you in all its detail and then receding behind you and nothing has any more significance than anything else: a stone in the road or the sun in your eyes or the black shape of a bird in the blue sky, you don't know whether one thing matters more than another?'

'Yes, it's often like that with me.'

'My mother's name was Calliope. Sometimes she sang a little song:

"Hermes the maybe, Hermes the sending –
in the day a road, in the night a wending."'

'"Who is Hermes?" I asked her.

'"Hermes is your father."

'"Where is he?"

'My mother pointed to the road. "Here and gone."

'"Where's Hermes?" I said to the shepherds.

'They showed me a heap of stones by the roadside. "There's Hermes," they said.

'"How can a heap of stones be Hermes?"

'"Every man who tupped your mother put a stone on that heap in the name of Hermes," they said.

'I put my ear to the stones, I listened to the dance in them, listened to the music of Hermes-in-the-stone. I looked at the road that was the place of Hermes. Without moving it ran through the valley and over the mountains, at the same time running and standing still, at the same time here and gone.

'That night I went to the road. There was no moon, only the

36

night and the dim road wending into darkness. I stamped on the road, I whispered, "Hermes!" The road moved backward under my feet, faster, faster. The steady rhythm of it stretched its long dream into the darkness and the whispering of the night. Running, running I said to the night "I have no name but the one you give me, no face but the one you see."

'I was, I am, an emptiness. I don't know what anything is: I don't know what music is, I don't know the difference between running and stillness, between dancing and death. The world vibrates like a crystal in the mind; there is a frequency at which terror and ecstasy are the same and any road may be taken. There was an olive grove, it was morning. Shadows and whispers in the greenlit shade and the sunlight twittering in the leaves above. Hermes doesn't show itself as a picture in the eyes, it's there like a beast that can't be seen, a strangeness dancing in the greenlit shade, dancing its music in the brightness of the shadows, in the darkness of the light.

'There was an olive grove, I could feel the Hermes of it. There was a tortoise. My hand reached down and picked up the tortoise; with a hiss it drew its head in. I stood there feeling the shape of it and the weight of it in my hand and there was an idea coming to me when I felt eyes on me, felt myself being looked at. There was someone else in the olive grove, there was a man who hadn't been there a moment ago. He was staring at me with eyes open so wide that I could see white all around the pupils. He had his hands out in front of him as if he was going to say, "Don't", but he didn't say anything. A dark man, not young, but I couldn't have said how old he was.

'The tortoise was in my left hand and my knife was in my right; my idea was the tortoise-shell empty and two posts and a yoke and some strings for a kind of little harp with the shell as a soundbox. The man's eyes were still on me, his wide-open eyes; almost I wanted to use the knife on him to make him stop looking at me. He let his hands drop to his sides when I cut the plastron loose and dug the body out of the shell, ugh! what a mess and my hands all slippery with blood and gore. The entrails were mysterious. I think about it now, how those entrails spilled out so easily when I made an emptiness for my music to sound in. Impossible to put those entrails back.

'You know how you'll hear a sound while you're asleep and

there comes a whole dream to account for it and in the dream there are things that happen before and after the sound – might it be that the whole universe has no purpose but to explain the killing of the tortoise? Do you see what I mean? Perhaps the universe is a continually fluctuating event that configures itself to whatever is perceived as centre. Do you think that might be how it is?'

I closed my eyes and saw the long nakedness of Luise twisting in the stardrift of galaxies and nebulae. 'I hope not,' I said.

'The dark man watched me as I emptied the tortoise-shell,' said the head. 'He cupped his hands in the shape of the shell, then he mimed the plucking of strings. "Music? For making music?" he said.

'"Yes, for making music," I said. "How did you know?" Because what I was going to do had never been done before, there was no such instrument as the lyre then.

'"I don't know how I know," he said. He had come closer; he smelled of honey.

'"Why do you smell of honey?" I said.

'"I keep bees." he said. "My name is Aristaeus." He stood there as if listening for something that only he could hear.

'"What are you listening for?" I said.

'"Your name."

I didn't say anything, I didn't want to tell him my name.

'"You don't want to tell it," he said. "You're afraid."

'"Afraid of what?" I said.

'"Afraid to hear the sound of your name in this place."

'"I'm not afraid."

'"Then tell it."

'"My name is Orpheus," I said. Still he seemed to be listening for something else. "What are you listening for now?" I said.

'"The olive trees whisper," he said. "I always listen. You are the one who is Orpheus."

'"I've just told you that."

'"Not just your name," he said. "You're going to do it, you're going to be Orpheus."

'"What else can I be?"

'"You are the story of yourself," he said. With his finger he traced figures in the air.

'"What's that you're doing?" I said.

'"Your name. You are the story of Orpheus."

'"How can I be a story? I'm a man, a live person."

'"You're a story."

'"Not a story," I said. I began to run.

'Behind me, even when I was far away, I heard him say quietly, "You're a story," and I wished I hadn't told him my name.' The head fell silent, I held it in my hands and waited.

'What happened next?' I said after a reasonable interval.

'My story is not a sequence of events like knots on a string,' said the head; 'I could have started with the loss of Eurydice and ended with the killing of the tortoise – all of it happens at once and it goes on happening; all of it is happening now and any part of it contains the whole of it, the pictures needn't be looked at in any particular order.'

'Why not?'

'Because the thing is simply what it is. Hold a pomegranate in your hand and tell me where is the beginning of it and where is the end. The name of this pomegranate is Loss: the loss of Eurydice was in me before I ever met her and the loss of me was in her the same.'

'Tell me what happened next.'

'After the making of the lyre there is a long empty space before I became the Orpheus who was said to charm wild beasts and move trees and stones. I assume that I very slowly taught myself to play the instrument, that I made up little songs, nothing special. Probably I sang and begged my way from place to place. When I try to think of myself in that time I think of an emptiness carrying the emptiness that had been the tortoise. There is no story of me for that time – what I had been was gone and what I was to be had not yet come.

'The next thing I know about is a morning, a dawn, the dawn mist rising from the river. I was sleeping off a drunk, I woke up not knowing who I was nor where I was. Something was looking at me from behind the mist, the strangeness that is Hermes, the strangeness that makes everything here and gone at the same time. The light changed and it was afternoon. The flight of the kingfisher opened in the air over the river a blue-green iridescent stillness in which a dragonfly, immense and transparent, repeated itself with every wingstroke. There was a drowsiness, a droning in the golden afternoon, a vibration in my mind or in the air, an ineffably sweet, honeyed sound that was seductive and demanding, a music not of any instrument. It enveloped and overwhelmed me, I felt myself surrendering to it, dying sweetly of it while the strangeness watched me from behind the blue-green stillness, from behind the dragonfly and the gold of the afternoon.

'The air itself seemed honeyed, and it was in that fragrance that I first heard her voice, the voice of the woman who became my story. I heard her weeping in the leafy shade while the dragonflies printed themselves gigantically on the transparent stillness over the river.

'There rose in my throat a terrible ache and in that moment the world became me and I became the world-child who knows nothing and believes whatever it is told; I was the world-child whose innocence binds the world together, whose innocence betrayed will unfasten the world. Oh yes, I thought, and as I listened to the weeping of the unseen woman in that golden, golden afternoon I became the tortoise I had killed. I felt my own cruel knife enter me, felt my life spurting out, felt my still quivering body being dug out of my shell. In an explosion of brilliant colours I suffered the many pains of death as underworld opened to me, underworld and the moment under the moment. I suffered the many pains, the many colours of death and I knew everything. The colours were swallowed up in blackness, there came a stillness and I found myself weeping by the river with the lyre in one hand and the plectrum in the other. The strings were still sounding as a song died on the air and I could feel in my throat that the singing had come from me but I could remember nothing of it. I tasted blood in my mouth and there was blood coming out of my nose. On both sides of the river the trees came down to the water's edge and swayed their tops against the sky.'

'There opened to you underworld,' I said, 'and you knew everything. I remember how it was, I remember her weeping.'

'Yes,' said the head, 'in the weeping of Eurydice there opened to me underworld.'

Here the voice of the head of Orpheus paused; the mottled sunlight and the leafy shade, the dragonflies and the river vanished into greyness. A desolation and a silence filled my mind. The sky was very pale. I wanted to keep the mottled sunlight and the leafy shade, the dragonflies, the honeyed air. I closed my eyes and waited for the voice to continue.

I heard the distant traffic on Putney Bridge, the rush of cars on the Lower Richmond Road. I opened my eyes. The water was lapping at my feet and the head was well out into the middle of the Thames moving downriver against the tide. I was surprised, I had expected the story to be finished in one telling. As I watched the head out of sight I felt abandoned and forlorn but there was no heart pain so I supposed in some way it was still with me.

6 We're not Talking about a Bloke with Winged Sandals

I came home feeling altogether used up and worn out but I typed up the whole episode while it was still fresh in my mind, put it on disk, and printed it out. On the far side of the common the plane trees swayed their tops against the morning sky. The telephone rang.

'Hello,' I said.

'Are you all right?' said Istvan Fallok. 'I tried to get you last night but your line was always engaged.'

'Why shouldn't I be all right?'

'You seemed to be in some kind of a state when you left here; you knocked me down and tore out of here with electrodes all over your head and you left your anorak behind. How are you feeling now?'

'I've just been chatting to a rotting head.'

'That isn't just any rotting head, it's the head of Orpheus.'

'So it tells me. Have you known each other long, you and it?'

'A year or so, I suppose, but I doubt that we'll be seeing each other again, it and I.'

'Why is that?'

'Did you have a little angina during your chat?'

'Yes, I did.'

'Did the head sing to you?'

'Yes, it did.'

'Did you hear anything?'

'No. Did you?'

'Yes. It sang in a barely audible sort of wheezing whisper and it did some supernaturally complex variations on a spooky theme for about twenty minutes. I kept thinking, Oh yes, I've got it, then the next moment I'd forgotten it. We were outdoors at the time, I'd no recording gear. When it finished it said to me, "There, you see?"

'"Could you sing it again?" I said. "I seem to have missed a lot of it."

42

'"Sing what?" it said.

'"What you just sang," I said.

'"Did I sing something?" it said.

'"Yes," I said, "just now."

'"I don't remember singing anything," it said. "Maybe if you give me the parts you remember we can put it together." So that's what we began to do. Every now and then the head would turn up and if we were at the studio I'd play what I'd done and we'd do a little more or if I was out somewhere I'd have a little keyboard with me. Month after month I worked on that music and I never could get it to come right, it just wouldn't hold still – I'd have a couple of minutes of it pretty well laid down and I'd think, well, now I've got something to work with, something I can develop; and then when I tried to develop it the whole thing fell apart like ropes of sand and I'd have to start all over again. Eventually I found myself in hospital with a myocardial infarction and I finally got some rest. It was wonderful, they let me stop there for a fortnight. Nurses are the nicest people there are; there was a lady who brought cups of tea at six in the morning and another with a book trolley and another with a little shop on wheels. They did ECGs and X-rays, tested my blood and my urine, recommended a low fat, low cholesterol diet, told me to take daily exercise and stop smoking, gave me a little bottle of glyceryl trinitrate tablets, and put me out on the street again.'

'How are you feeling now?'

'Now that I've put the head on to you I feel terrific.'

'You've never forgiven me for Luise, have you?'

'Did you expect me to?'

'She was leaving you anyhow; if it hadn't been me it would've been somebody else.'

'And if it weren't the head of Orpheus bothering you now it'd be something else.'

'What happened after you got out of hospital? Did you see the head again?'

'I was hoping not to but a kind of madness came on me and I bought a large Edam cheese and when I took it out of the bag there was the head of Orpheus continuing its variations on the same spooky theme. I dropped it off Westminster Bridge at three o'clock in the morning and stuck a flyer through your letterbox.'

'You haven't told me how you first met the head of Orpheus.'

'It started with the Hermes music. The client said it didn't sound like foot powder and of course he was right; it wasn't foot-powder music, it was straight Hermes. Foot powder was what I was honestly trying for but what I got was the thief-god, the god of roadways and night journeys, the god of here-and-gone, the easer through the shadows, the finder in the dark. Hermes is like that, you know: it'll do as it likes.'

'You say "it" not "he".'

'Well, we're not talking about a bloke with winged sandals and a staff with two snakes twined around it, are we.'

'What are we talking about?'

'Obviously it's nothing you can see: it's a mode of event, a shift in the relativities of the moment, a new disposition of energies. There's what you might call a frequency of probability when complementary equivalents offer and anything can be anything.'

'For example?'

'Like all of a sudden you could be Luise's lover and I could be out.'

'Ah.'

'That's one word for it.'

'And you're saying that's Hermes?'

'Hermes acting on a certain kind of material.'

'And how did the head of Orpheus come into it?'

'I'd been in the kind of state you're in now – I'd been trying to get to places in my head I hadn't been to before. I was fooling around with sonically configured EEG enhancement and I tried the Hermes music with it. When I had a nice alpha rhythm going and some interesting frequencies from some of the electrodes I tried jump-starting my head with capacitor discharges; I upped the voltage in easy stages with a 50-microsecond time constant until it put me where I saw the head of Orpheus. I saw it far away on a calm and shining sea and I was swimming towards it but I never got any closer. Later I went to Berwick Street and there it was on a barrow amongst some melons. I've got to ring off now. Don't forget to pick up your anorak and please bring the electrodes with you.'

'Plus the fifty pounds I didn't pay you yesterday.'

'Forget it, this one's on me.'

'No it isn't, it's on me now.'

'That's how it goes. Has the head had much to say to you so far?'

'It's begun to tell me its story.'

'Ah, it would do, wouldn't it. Music with me and a story with you. Well, good luck with it,' and he rang off.

A low panic thrilled along the wires of my nervous system. The day was becoming hard and sunny with a high wind blowing the brown leaves against the wire mesh fence of the football pitch. The District Line trains rumbled past westbound to Parsons Green, Putney Bridge, Wimbledon, eastbound to Upminster, Tower Hill, Dagenham East with passengers, the sea, mountains and death. I looked at the postcard of the Vermeer girl. Afraid but seeking to avert nothing Luise looked back at me in the November daylight. The first time I saw that look on her face was about seven o'clock on a Sunday morning at the house in Kilburn where she had the bedsit. It was a few days after our first evening together, we hadn't yet made love; I'd kissed her and she smelled of honey, she said it was cough sweets. I'd been thinking about her all the time so I drove up there and rang her bell. She came to the door in pyjamas, no eyebrows, and that look that sought to avert nothing but was questioning, uncertain, and afraid. What was there to be afraid of?

We went up to her room and she made coffee. On the wall was an old clock she'd brought with her from Germany, it was stopped. It had a round wooden case and a sad white face with delicate black roman numerals. I opened the back and released the escapement; the works unwound with a great whirring; then I wound it up and started it running again. When she came to live with me in Fulham its pale white moonface rose over our lovemaking, over the smooth and shining sea of our pleasure. Then it stopped and wouldn't go again however much I tinkered with it. There wasn't a wall in our bedroom that clock was happy on; it hung there staring with its pendulum dead and the little door at the bottom of the case dropped open like the jaw of a skeleton.

My unfinished adaptation of *Dracula* lay on the desk. I opened the folder and looked at where I'd left off:

DOWN AMONG THE SHADOWY TOMBS PROFESSOR VAN HELSING OPENS THE COFFIN OF ONE OF THE VAMPIRE BRIDES OF DRACULA . . .

Van Helsing: How beautiful she is in her Vampire sleep!

In her silk-lined coffin Melanie Falsepercy, the Vermeer girl, lay with her eyes open, her red lips slightly parted, her long hair loose about her. Van Helsing's speech balloon throbbed with the old man's lust.

The telephone rang. I picked it up and said hello.

'Herman?' said the voice of Sol Mazzaroth. His damp and sweaty hand came out of the telephone and touched my arm.

'I should have *Dracula* wound up tonight,' I said. 'Van Helsing's down among the tombs now finishing off the vampire ladies.'

'Not to worry,' said Mazzaroth. 'You've got time on that. Can you come in tomorrow afternoon around half-past three? I've got something really exciting to tell you.'

'OK, I'll be there.'

I switched on the radio and got Radio Moscow at 12020 kHz with Alla Pugachova singing *Harlekino*. Is there a story of me? I asked myself. Am I in it? I typed:

SOME DRAMATIS PERSONAE IN ORDER OF APPEARANCE

The Kraken, the underhead: by its own account it came into existence when the human mind needed another mind to hold the original terror but it may well be of earlier origin. Eurydice claims to be its mother by a giant squid.

Eurydice, mother? of the Kraken; the vast and ivory nakedness of her rising from the deeps. Luise von Himmelbett and Melanie Falsepercy are the Eurydice of this story, the lost one, the gone one, the one who cannot stay.

Dike or *Dice* is Justice or Natural Law. Eurydice is Wide Justice, justice everywhere, universal natural law. What, the loss of her?

The Giant Squid, an aspect of Orpheus, also (in a non-gigantic way) of Orff. Lusting after fishergirls.

The Vermeer Girl, an aspect of the Mother Goddess, the female principle that manifests itself as Eurydice or Persephone or Luise or Melanie Falsepercy or Medusa. I have in mind the face of the composite Eurydice loosely grinning, becoming, becoming . . . ?

The Olive Tree, Luise and I called it a Persephone door but mainly it's the flickering of Thing-in-Itself.

Apple II,
Drake R7,   } aspects of the Olive Tree
The District Line,

The Head of Orpheus, the overhead. It isn't to be trusted, I know that: music with Fallok and a story with me, and the one likely to end up as badly as the other. All the same I have to trust it – we're in this together, it and I, for as long as it continues to think of me.

Aristaeus, what is he in the story, why is he being so pretentiously The Mysterious Stranger? Is there something about him that reminds me of people who get there before I do, who know something I don't know? Or is it simply that he's an inconvenient witness to the killing of the tortoise? Why am I afraid that he'll take something away from me?

Here the DRAMATIS PERSONAE came to an end. I had lunch and a kip, stuck the *Dracula* disk in the Apple II, turned on the monitor, and sank into a reverie.

The afternoon immersed itself in dusk and the dusk deepened into night. District Line trains with golden windows rumbled townwards and homewards; the football pitch was illuminated, the lower leaves of the plane trees on the common became brilliant and theatrical; I heard the cries of the players, the thudding of the ball as the figures moved under the chalky whiteness of the lights; along the footpaths on either side of the pitch homegoers passed with quickened footsteps. I looked at the Vermeer girl, saw Melanie Falsepercy, remembered Luise. In the window my lamplit face was reflected on the darkness; I pulled down the blinds and saw the following appear on the monitor as I typed:

47

The sea is full of marvels but there are no answers in it. There are remote beaches where certain things are insisted upon. There are crabs whose bodies are like human faces, angry and disappointed faces with mouth parts gabbling silently, urgently. These faces are carried on jointed legs, they hurry along the tidal edge drivenly surviving from one moment to the next; there is no time to lose if their line of angry and disappointed faces is to continue.

In the spring tides the female crab releases her ten thousand eggs, each one a potential angry and disappointed face and most of them will be eaten by the creatures of the sea. The female stands not like a face on legs, she stands huge, heroic and technological, like a spacecraft poised on elaborately articulated legs; she stands like the most modern thing in the world and she expels into the sea these ten thousand ancient faces.

There's no end to me, no limit, no way to define or measure me, no way of knowing what I am or how much of me there is. There is an endless surging and undulating of me, an endless cycle of ebb and flow: that is called the sea. Little moments of me have lines drawn before and after and these moments are given names like Orpheus and Eurydice and they become stories. But I am wordless, heaving in the ocean night of me, stirring in the dark trees, breathing in and breathing out my soul.

I resumed the unfinished *Dracula* page. Van Helsing drove a stake into the heart of the beautiful vampire. NNYURG-HLLGHHhhaaaaah! shrieked the Vermeer girl.

7   Nnngghh, Zurff, Kruljjj

When I arrived at *Classic Comics* the next afternoon I noticed a
little more liveliness, a little more motion in the place than
usual; there was that unmistakable quickening that comes
with the smell of new business. In Sol Mazzaroth's office I saw
a full-page four-colour proof of an old newspaper ad for
Orpheus Men's Toiletries pinned up on the corkboard.
They'd reproduced the pastel drawing by Redon with the
golden lyre-head of Orpheus, the blue-green lyre, the golden
mountainscape, the violet sky. Overlapping a corner of the
Redon was a photograph of a chunky amphora-shaped imi-
tation clay bottle with pseudo-Greek letters incised on it.
CLASSIQUE: ETERNAL MAGIC BY ORPHEUS, said the headline I'd
written years ago.

'Takes you back, doesn't it,' said Mazzaroth.

'I don't want to be taken back,' I said.

'It's all happening,' he said, swivelling excitedly in his black
leather chair. 'We're going glossy and we're merging with *He*.
No more of this kid shit with one-inch single-column ads for
catapults and model steam engines – we're talking full-page
four-colour Yves St Laurent and Alpha Romeo and Orpheus.
What I want to do now is get into real classics, I mean your
actual Greek ones, I don't know why I never thought of it
before. This is a chance to broaden and deepen our para-
meters.' He picked up a copy of *Lemprière's Classical Dictionary*. 'Listen to this:

> . . . the Thracian women, whom he had offended by his
> coldness to their amorous passion, or, according to others,
> by his unnatural gratifications and impure indulgences,
> attacked him while they celebrated the orgies of Bacchus,
> and after they had torn his body to pieces, they threw his
> head into the Hebrus, where it still articulated the words
> 'Eurydice! Eurydice!' as it was carried down the stream
> into the Aegean Sea.

49

'That's what I call a story with possibilities,' he said. 'I want you to work this up into something we can run as a serial in the first six issues.'

'There's not a lot to work up, is there,' I said. 'All we know about Orpheus is what a great musician he was and how Eurydice was bitten by a snake while being chased by Aristaeus and she died and Orpheus went to the underworld to bring her back and so on.'

'Come on, Herman, this is an X-rated magazine. You can easily get one instalment out of the Thracian women and their amorous passion and another out of the unnatural gratifications. And of course there's Eurydice and all that underworld action, maybe a big fight between Orpheus and Hades before he gets her out of there. Or maybe Persephone gets the hots for him and there's a heavy scene with her, there's no end to the underworld possibilities. You'll think of something good to start it off, like how he gets the magic lyre, maybe some thunder and lightning on a mountaintop or he's got to wrestle somebody for it or kill a monster or whatever. This isn't going to be some little wimp Orpheus, what we want is a really hunky guy, we'll use Pektoralis for the art, he'll give it that heroic sci-fi look. And we're not doing it comic-style, either – no speech balloons, it's going to be strictly quality stuff with the text under the pictures. Here, have a look at the dummy.'

CLASSIQUE, it said on the cover in pseudo-Greek lettering. The cover photo was a bronzed youth leaping out of the sea with shining drops of water scattering from him. Over the sky and the water were listed the contents:

CRUISING THE AEGEAN
THE TREATS OF SAN FRANCISCO
AIDS: GHETTO OF FEAR
GREAT SALADS OF THE WORLD
GÖSTA KRAKEN, EYE OF DARKNESS
ORPHEUS: SIX-PART PICTURE SERIES

'Gösta Kraken,' I said. 'Didn't he do a film called *Quagmires*?'

'*Bogs*,' said Sol. 'He's the hottest thing since Tarkovsky. His latest film is *Codename Orpheus*. What do you think of the dummy?'

'Looks glossy.'

'*Classique*, same as the after-shave. Orpheus is running a special full page.' He opened the dummy to it. There was a detail of the Redon drawing but most of the page was taken up by a discreetly shadowy photograph of two nude men.

CLASSIQUE BY ORPHEUS:
MAGIC EVER NEW FROM THE GOLDEN AGE

'How does that grab you?' he said.

'NNNGGHH,' I said. 'ZURFF, KRULJJJ.'

'It's a big, big market; this merger is going to mean a five million increase in circulation and an estimated twelve million pounds in advertising revenue. What it means for you is four big ones.'

'Four thousand pounds!' I was only getting six hundred for *Dracula*.

'You're in the big time now and it's only the beginning. Theseus and the Minotaur — what really happened in the labyrinth, eh? Talk about unnatural practices. Pasiphaë and the bull before that, naturally. But first let's get Orpheus off the ground.'

'Or on it, face down.'

'That's it. I'm going to need your finished adaptation in a month so give this your best upmarket thinking and get back to me in the next couple of days with your outline.'

'Sol,' said his classically endowed secretary, 'I have Kuwait for you.'

Mazzaroth squeezed my hand. 'We'll talk soon, OK? Let's have lunch.'

'What about *Dracula*? I finished it this morning.'

He took the envelope from me. 'This'll run in the last issue of *Classic Comics*. Ciao.'

'Bye-bye,' said his secretary, her name was Kim. I found myself in the waiting-room looking up at the Calder that stirred silently like speech balloons from God. I was going down in the lift; the doors opened; the building was behind me; the sounds of High Holborn closed around me; I was out in the street feeling unlucky and walking in such a manner that oncoming pedestrians found me opposing them like a mirror image, sidestepping with them in perfect synchrony to do the same

51

again. I sensed that something that until now had taken no notice of me had slowly lifted up its head and was watching me. There leaped into my mind those lines from 'The Rime of the Ancient Mariner':

> Like one, that on a lonesome road
> Doth walk in fear and dread,
> And having once turn'd round walks on,
> And turns no more his head;
> Because he knows, a frightful fiend
> Doth close behind him tread.

Then of course my cruel picture-shuffling mind gave me Luise as an albatross soaring on a boundless marine sky. There was a leaden feeling in my arms and in my chest; I wished from the bottom of my heart that Sol Mazzaroth had never mentioned Orpheus to me.

In the underground I looked up and found the pseudo-Greek ORPHEUS TRAVEL card staring at me. The light in the carriage was like the light in someone else's bathroom when you're sick at a party.

Trying to walk naturally and be invisible I surfaced at Oxford Circus and made my way to Istvan Fallok's Piranesi corner of Soho. There he was in his electronic twilight with his veiled music going and all his little eyes glowing their different colours around him in the dusk.

'How's it going?' he said.

'It's too soon to say.' I gave him the electrodes and the wires and a cheque for fifty pounds and he tore up the cheque and gave me my anorak.

'Want a coffee?' he said.

'Not now, thanks.' I almost said, 'I'm being followed.'

'You look as if you were about to say something.'

'I often look that way. I'll be going now. See you.'

'See you,' said Fallok, and receded into his musical twilight.

8 Tower Hill and the Cheshire Cheese

When I got home I sat at my desk but I couldn't bear the thought of making words appear on the screen. I looked up Orpheus in the telephone directory. There were only Orpheus Travel in the Fulham Road, Orpheus Wines, Impt & Whlslrs in SE16, and the Orpheus & Tower Bridge Club in Savage Gardens, EC3.

Savage Gardens! I dialled the number and after four or five rings a woman answered, 'Orpheus and Tower Bridge Club; can I help you?' In the background I could hear the clatter of cutlery and crockery.

'Can you tell me what sort of a club it is?' I said.

'It's a members' club.' She sounded busy.

'You mean, people just come there to eat and drink?'

'Yes, it's just a members' club.'

'There's no musical activity of any kind?'

'Oh no, nothing like that.'

'How does one become a member?'

'There's a form to fill in.'

'Haven't I got to be proposed by somebody?'

'Oh yes, you've got to be proposed and seconded by members of the club.'

'I don't know anybody who's a member.'

'What company or firm are you with?'

'I'm not with anyone, I'm a freelance writer.'

'Just a minute.' She consulted briefly with someone. 'Yes, that's all right. Come along.'

'What are your hours?'

'We're here from nine to seven.'

'You don't do suppers then.'

'Oh no, we only do lunches.'

The idea of a club of people eating lunches was frightening to me. Orphic action seemed unlikely in such a setting. Still, I thought, a place called Savage Gardens must have significance.

I looked it up in my *A to Z*. It was just by the Tower Hill tube station, close to Trinity House and Trinity Square, near Seething Lane, Hart Street, and Crutched Friars. South of it were the river and Tower Bridge.

I left the house at about five o'clock. It was novembering hard outside; the dark air sang with the dwindle of the year, the sharpening of it to the goneness that was drawing nearer, nearer with every moment. Pinky-orange shone the electrical-hibiscus street lamps; almost their light had a fragrance; the brown leaves underfoot insisted on the ghosts of dark trees standing in the place of lamps and houses; the pinky-orange globes hung mingled with the swaying dark and winter branches; the winter lights and traffic, the winter walkers in the dark street all moved through the ghostly wood and went their way upon the ancient leafy track.

Fulham Broadway station, its platforms half indoors, half out in the weather and the winter dark, was lit up and festive looking, the people moving down the stairs to the platforms seemed each of them the forward edge of a fascinating story urgent to be told. The first train was an Edgware Road one; I got on and changed to an Upminster train at Earl's Court.

The train rumbled eastward through the evening. People surged on and off, each face sharp and clear and undeniably of the present moment. At every station I felt more responsive, as if a slider on a rheostat was advancing with the train: Sloane Square, Victoria, St James's Park, Westminster, Embankment, Temple, Blackfriars, Mansion House, Cannon Street, Monument . . .

Tower Hill! With others I poured out of the train in a many-legged movement up the stairs into the bright darkness and the smell of roasting chestnuts and the purposeful rush towards us of homegoers from the offices all around, their faces strong with evening and November, sharp and clear with actuality under the pinky-orange hibiscus lamps, under the wild sky and the dark tower by the running of the dark and shining river.

Past Trinity Square I went, looking up at the dim whiteness of the Port of London Authority with its columns and its statue that was now obscure in its niche, the building fabulous against the dark sky like an Edmund Dulac mosque. I turned into

54

Savage Gardens, full moons in my mind and innocent mystic lions by the Douanier Rousseau. No moon, no lions. I continued past Trinity House with its elegant lantern, past new brick and stone rising from the old. On one of the old brick arches of the railway bridge to Fenchurch Street Station I saw black lettering on a white background: The Orpheus & Tower Bridge Club. The club itself was on the near side of the railway bridge, just beyond Ye Olde Englishe Clubbe. Through the arch of the bridge the Cheshire Cheese was visible.

The entrance to the Orpheus & Tower Bridge Club was a modest glass door like that of a small hotel. By then I understood that the main fact of this particular evening was the novembering of it, the pinky-orange hibiscus lamplight, the clear bright darkness between the lamps, the smell of roasting chestnuts, the coming to a point of the dwindling year; I went past the door without stopping, I didn't want to fill in a form.

Before me the bridge loomed great-arched, great-shadowed, high in the lonesome evening, waiting like a stage set while the trains rumbled over it into and out of Fenchurch Street. In Crutched Friars in the darkness under the bridge the Cheshire Cheese stood dimly and invited with its golden windows. It looked not too lively, not too bright, decently tired. A sign on the door warned that:

PERSONS WITH
DIRTY CLOTHES, BOOTS, OR SHOES
WILL NOT BE SERVED HERE.

I went into the public bar, a commodious and quiet place in which black-shaded spotlights hanging from a high and shadowy black ceiling stared down at carpeting with a geometric pattern of a floral sort in various tones of red. Red glass-shaded lamps on the walls gave a warm light to the tables, the banquettes, the carpeting, the sitting and standing figures, that warmth reaching only to a certain height where it yielded to the downward-reaching shadows of the black ceiling and the sparse glare of the black-shaded spotlights. Between the ascending red and the descending black the murmur of the drinkers made an invisible shelter, a canopy of overlapping quiet voices. From the saloon bar were heard cheering and

55

shouts and high-spirited conversation, but this part of the Cheshire Cheese was of a more subdued and thoughtful character. A man in a blue short-sleeved shirt went about gathering up beer mugs and glasses, occasionally speaking with an accent so regional that it used up all his articulation and left nothing over for words. 'Gom yawncher!' he said to a man at one of the tables.

'Aye,' said the other, 'it's always the same.'

Two old coughers nearby stopped coughing, rolled fresh cigarettes, lit them, inhaled, started coughing again.

As the gom yawncher man passed me I recognized him as the man in the broken-brimmed hat who'd spoken to me in the underground when I was on my way home from Istvan Fallok's studio with electrodes all over my head.

'Hello,' I said.

'Nimser vo,' he said.

'You weren't talking like that the other day. How come?'

'I must've been somebody else then.'

'How's that?'

'Economy. You have a little chat with a stranger now and then, right? So do I, so does everyone. How many lines has the stranger got? Two or three maybe. There's really no need for a new actor each time, is there.'

'So you play them all.'

'The same as you.'

'What do you mean?'

'Yesterday you were the conductor on the 11 bus and you also did quite a nice little tobacconist in the Charing Cross Road. Actually London hasn't got that big a cast, there's only about fifty of us, all working flat out.'

'Are you writing a novel?'

'Novel-writing is for weaklings,' he said, and moved on.

I went to the bar, got a half-pint of bitter and a large whisky, found myself a table and sank into a deep quietude.

Near me a young man was showing photographs to a young woman. From the position of their knees I guessed that this must be an early stage of their acquaintance. The banquette on which they sat ran north-east and south-west; his knees faced east without touching her south-facing ones while she bent over the photographs with polite interest. Well, I thought, they

56

have it all before them, and there was a surge of sadness and longing in me.

When I looked around again I saw Melanie Falsepercy just taking off her coat as she sat down in a corner by one of the red-shaded lamps. Her face seemed to have been called up on the evening air by the hibiscus lamplight, the clear bright darkness, the smell of roasting chestnuts, the winter-sharp woodland of the year that she brought in with her. Istvan Fallok was with her; without seeing me he sat down with his back to me.

She hadn't noticed me. I moved around to the other side of the table so that my back was to her and Fallok. All of it is happening now, I thought, and any part of it contains the whole of it, the pictures needn't be looked at in any particular order. I turned around and found Melanie Falsepercy looking straight at me. I looked away, finished my drink quickly, and slunk out of the Cheshire Cheese without looking back.

9 The Thinking Man's Cabbage

The morning after seeing Melanie Falsepercy and Istvan
Fallok at the Cheshire Cheese I crossed Putney Bridge at a little
after seven and went to the place where the head had first
appeared to me.

The sky grew pale, a crow flew over the river, shouting and
flaunting its blackness.

'Head of Orpheus,' I said, 'are you there?'

Nothing in the river but the boats at their moorings, nothing
on the shore but me. Traffic hissing and rushing over the
bridge and on the Lower Richmond Road. I could feel that it
was going to be one of those hard blue-sky sunny days and my
heart sank.

'Sol Mazzaroth wants me to do an upmarket Orpheus story,'
I said, 'but I don't want to do it. I want to hear what you have to
tell me, we have to finish your story.'

Nothing. A second crow flew over the river shouting and
flaunting like the other. A third crow followed the second. The
sky was hard and blue like painted steel.

'Thank you very much indeed,' I said, and went home.

'Mr Orff?' said the telephone.

'This is we.'

'I have a call for you from Sol Mazzaroth,' said the voice of
the *Classic Comics* telephonist. Her name was Lucretia and she
was a perfectly respectable woman of fifty or so whose voice
had in it just the slightest hint of high boots and a whip.

'Hi, Sol,' I said.

'Just a moment,' she said, 'I haven't put him on yet.'

'Ring me back when he's on then,' I said, and hung up.

Ring, ring, said the telephone.

'Good morning,' I said. 'I have a call for Sol Mazzaroth from
Herman Orff.'

'I was just calling you,' said Lucretia. 'I have Sol Mazzaroth
for you.'

'Hi, Sol.'

'Just a moment, please,' she said.

'Then you haven't really got him, have you.' I hung up again. This time I took the phone off the hook.

After a while I rang up Istvan Fallok. Behind him I heard the Hermes music again. 'Listen,' I said, 'I need another fix.'

'I don't know.'

'What do you mean you don't know?'

'The way you freaked out the first time, there's no telling what a second jolt might trigger off. And for all I know I could be had up for practising EEG without a licence.'

'You're the one that got me hooked. Don't chicken out on me now.'

'You've got funny ideas about what constitutes chickening out. Some people might say you were chickening out when you tried to get a novel out of your head with a machine.'

'At least I'm man enough not to lay off the Orpheus action on somebody else and give them angina.'

'Then I'm sure you're man enough to carry on alone. Now if you don't mind I have to get back to what I'm doing.'

'Don't we all,' I said as I stared at the wordless monitor.

THINK OF ME AS I THINK OF YOU, said the Kraken.

Last time you didn't want me to think of you. You were afraid you might be real.

I AM REAL. I KNOW NOW THAT IT IS NOT POSSIBLE TO EXIST WITHOUT BEING REAL. THINK OF ME.

Why do you want me to think of you?

I WANT TO BE MORE REAL.

Why?

IT'S IN THE NATURE OF THINGS.

I do think of you. I have always thought of you, I've told you that before.

HOW HAVE YOU THOUGHT OF ME? WHAT IS THE FORM OF ME IN YOUR THOUGHTS?

I told you that the first time we spoke.

TELL ME AGAIN.

I think of you as the great cephalopod, ancient of the deeps. I think of you as the great thinking head in the blackness of the ultimate deep, I think of you as the Kraken.

AND THE LITTLE CHILDREN? YOU SPOKE OF LITTLE CHILDREN THE FIRST TIME.

Even little children have an idea of you in their minds. They draw a great head with all the limbs growing out of it.

VAST AND WRITHING.

Actually they mostly draw your limbs thin and gangling.

BUT I AM VAST AND WRITHING.

Yes, of course.

WHEN DID YOU BEGIN TO THINK OF ME?

For as long as my mind has been you have been in my mind. Always have I heard the circles of your terror widening in the deeps but it was the head of Orpheus I wanted to talk to really.

YOU KNOW THAT I'M THE UNDERHEAD, I'M DEEPER THAN THE HEAD OF ORPHEUS.

Yes. I have to go out now. We'll talk soon.

I switched off the monitor. Whenever the Kraken and I spoke in words on the screen I experienced a surge of terror at the centre of me that was comfortable and familiar, I felt as if I'd always known the Kraken and I knew that we always told each other the truth. With the head of Orpheus things were always awkward and it was by its own admission unreliable but I felt a strong need to talk to it. I couldn't think of any reason to go out but there weren't any bananas in the house so I went to the North End Road market.

'Look, look!' shouted a man. 'Look at this cabbage! Get yourself a head, you never know when you'll need one!' It was the gom yawncher man from the Cheshire Cheese who'd also been the broken-brimmed-hat man in the underground. 'Look, look!' he shouted.

I looked. There it was, green-slimed and barnacled among the lawful fruit and vegetables on the barrow. Its mouth was open and speaking. 'Swaying, swaying their tops against the sky the trees came down to the water's edge,' said the head of Orpheus, 'and I found her there in the mottled sunlight and the leafy shade by the river.'

'For God's sake,' I said, 'not here!' To the gom yawncher man I said, 'I'll have this one.'

'Sixty-five p for the thinking man's cabbage head,' he said as he weighed it and wrapped it up in page three of the *Sun*, 'with a visual treat thrown in.'

'You remember me, don't you?' I said. 'From the underground and the Cheshire Cheese?'

60

'How could I forget?' he said.

As I hurried home through the people and the traffic the head continued its story. I had to hold it close to my ear to hear what it was saying, 'In the leafy shade she lay all huddled and forlorn, the red-gold hair, the ivory of her in the cool and leafy shade by the river, her garments all disordered offering to the eye her shapeliness, her long and rounded limbs; splendid and sculptural she was, like a broken winged victory. The honeyed air droned and sang; the ivory of her, the pathetic and savage splendour of her beauty sang in my eyes as I knelt beside her. Gone she was and lost to me for ever, Eurydice! Eurydice!'

'What on earth are you talking about?' I said. 'How can she be gone and lost to you for ever when you haven't even met her yet?'

'Where was I?' said the head. 'Where did I leave off last time?'

'You heard the unseen woman weeping by the river and you became the world-child and the tortoise you'd killed. Underworld opened to you and you sang and blood came out of your mouth and your nose.'

'Yes. Weeping, weeping in the golden afternoon her voice came to me in the mottled sunlight by the river and I went to where she lay all huddled and forlorn, the red-gold hair, the ivory of her in the cool and leafy shade by the river, her garments all disordered offering to the eye her shapeliness, her long and rounded limbs; splendid and sculptural she was, like a broken winged victory. The honeyed air droned and sang, the ivory of her, the pathetic and savage splendour of her beauty sang in my eyes as I knelt beside her. She looked at me not as one looks at a stranger but as if she expected me to comfort her. Full of desire and uncertainty I took her in my arms. She smelled of honey, it was like a dream, there was no strangeness in it; there already seemed to be a long history between us.' The head lapsed into silence.

'Go on,' I said.

'Go on with what?'

'With what happened when you found Eurydice weeping in the leafy shade.'

'We made love.'

61

'Didn't you say anything first? Surely you didn't just jump on her without a word?'

'I don't know what I said at first.'

'You probably said, "Why are you crying?"'

'That was it,' said the head. 'I said, "Why are you crying?"

'"I was sleeping," she said, "and I dreamed that I was the whole world; the whole world had become me and I was a child and I was afraid." She was still trembling as she clung to me.

'"Did you hear me singing by the river?" I said.

'"In my dream there came around me all the strange and many colours of death," she said. "They took my hands and wanted me to dance with them and I was afraid."' Here again the head fell silent.

'Well,' I said, 'what did you say to that?'

'I kissed her,' said the head. 'She tasted of honey.'

'"You taste of blood," she said.

'"Something happened in my throat when I sang," I said. But again she ignored my mention of the singing. I don't remember what she said after that.'

'Yes, you do.'

'It hurts to remember.'

'Yes, but without remembering we have nothing.'

'She said, "Be the world-child with me,"' said the head.

At that moment some large schoolboys lurched violently into me, I dropped the head, and one of the boys kicked it into the road. Several cars passed before I could go after it, and by then there was no sign of it anywhere.

10   All Hallows by the Tower

I spent the rest of the day typing up everything so far which brought me to this page. Several times the telephone rang and I could hear Lucretia stamping her booted foot inside it but I didn't answer.

In the evening, the evening after seeing Melanie Falsepercy and Istvan Fallok at the Cheshire Cheese, I went there again. I arrived a little after seven; that was about the time they'd come in. I sat down at the same table I'd sat at before and placed myself so as to have a good view of the door.

In my mind she arrived at a quarter past seven, smiled tentatively and looked at me with her woodland look as I stood up. She came over to the table, I pulled out a chair for her and helped her out of her coat. I was overwhelmed by the actuality of her. Like Luise she was taller than I; she smelled of youth and miracles, of November darkness and hibiscus lamplight.

Hello, she said as she sat down in my mind in the chair that stood empty before me. Here I am. Did you think I'd come?

The gom yawncher man, making his rounds, smiled at me and said, 'Numsy fy?'

'It's too soon to say,' I said. 'It's all in my mind.' I went out into Crutched Friars, turned right, turned left, followed a sign that pointed to St Olave's Church, crossed a big road full of blackness and white headlamps, fetched up at All Hallows by the Tower and went inside.

It seemed a working church in good order, and the many models in the Mariners' Chapel in the south aisle gave it a pleasantly practical air. There was a Communion service going on but a sign in the south aisle indicated that one might pray privately in the Chapel of St Francis in the crypt.

Going down the stairs I came first to the tiny dim Oratory of St Clare in which were two chairs and two prie-dieux facing a small Romanesque window with a grille in front of it. Beyond the window in a lighted alcove was an unlit brass oil lamp of the sort that Aladdin rubbed. This one stood on a rather tall foot and the handle of it was in the form of the chi-rho monogram. I sat down in one of the chairs and mentally rubbed the lamp.

There was a clip-clopping on the staircase and a stirring in the air, winter-sharp and woodlandish.

'Hello,' said Melanie Falsepercy as she sat down beside me. 'Here I am. Did you think I'd come?'

Thank you, I said to the lamp. 'I wasn't expecting you at All Hallows,' I said to her.

'I followed you here from the Cheshire Cheese,' she said.

'I didn't see you when I was there.'

'I was outside standing under the bridge, skulking in the shadows.'

'But why didn't you come in?'

'It wasn't coming-in time, it was skulking-in-the-shadows time.'

'And then you followed me here.'

'Because I'd been waiting for you.'

A prayerful-looking man entered the oratory. We left, went out of the church, and stood hand in hand before the big road of blackness and white headlamps.

'You'd been waiting for me,' I shouted against the rushing of the blackness and the lights.

She brought her mouth close to my ear. 'Yes,' she said.

We crossed the road, the rushing faded behind us. Great-arched, great-shadowed, high in the lonesome evening the railway bridge loomed before us, the golden windows of the Cheshire Cheese invited. We entered the ascending red, the descending black and found ourselves a table under the canopy of quiet voices.

'What're you having?' I said.

'Whatever you're having.'

I got us both treble gins with just a little water.

'Gin looks so clear,' she said, 'and it's so full of obscurity. Here's to All Hallows.'

'All Hallows. It was very strange yesterday evening; all of a sudden there you were.'

'I'd never been here before. Had you?'

'Never. What brought you?'

'I'd been translating Rilke's 'Orpheus, Eurydike, Hermes' and then I looked up Orpheus in the telephone directory.

When I saw the Orpheus and Tower Bridge Club listing I had to come to Savage Gardens for a look round. Thirsty work.'

Luise had translated that poem for me, I'd recorded her reading it in German and in English and I still remembered lines here and there:

> Wie eine Frucht von Süßigkeit und Dunkel,
> so war sie voll von ihrem großen Tode . . .

> Like a fruit of sweetness and darkness,
> So was she full of her large death . . .

'Do you do a lot of translation?' I said.

'No, it just happened that I wanted to get the ideas in the poem as clear in my mind as I could.'

'Do you do any writing?'

'Bits and pieces, nothing I'd show anyone yet.'

'And you and Fallok?'

'Not any more but we have a drink together now and then. What brought you to Savage Gardens?'

'A conversation with the head of Orpheus.'

'How did you and it meet?'

'I hallucinated it in the mud at low tide near Putney Bridge.'

'You and Tycho Fremdorf.'

'Who's Tycho Fremdorf?'

'Haven't you seen Codename Orpheus?'

'No. Why?'

'Better now?' said the gom yawncher man as he cleared the table.

'Much better, thanks,' I said.

'I keep seeing that man in different places,' I said to Melanie when he'd gone.

'That happens to Tycho Fremdorf too,' she said.

'What is all this about Tycho Fremdorf?'

'Tycho Fremdorf is the protagonist of Codename Orpheus. He's a sort of alienated anti-hero film-maker. He's been wandering around all night with his Arriflex and in the dawn we see him standing in the low-tide mud near the Albert Bridge. Everything still and grey and the boats rocking at their moorings and then he sees the head of Orpheus coming up the river against the tide. It's quite remarkable, there was a long piece about the film in *Sight and Sound*. Are you all right?'

'What do you mean? Why shouldn't I be all right?'

'You look very pale.'

'I always look pale. What did they say about *Codename Orpheus*, in *Sight and Sound*?'

'Sylvestre Lyzée wrote the piece; he said that it worked on the deconstructionist level but he had a little trouble with the reality-frame.'

'Wasn't it directed by what was his name, Gustav Krähe?'

'Gösta Kraken.'

'He's the one where it's always very dark and you often see people lying in puddles, isn't he? Didn't he do a film called *Squelchy Places*?'

'*Bogs*. In this one he goes in for rivers and low-tide mud a lot. The look of it is really terrific, that shot of the head coming up the Thames against the tide stays in the mind like some of Eisenstein's images. It isn't like the head of a swimming man, it's all rotting and bloated and eyeless and it has this awful stillness about it as it moves upriver.'

I'd brought with me the pages I'd typed so far and at some point I'd put the folder on the table. There it lay in the shadow of *Codename Orpheus*. I put it back in my shoulder bag.

'You brought a typescript with you and now you've put it away,' she said. 'Why'd you do that?'

'This night is different from other nights,' I said. As I said it I had the sensation of rocking in the sea and feeling something rising dark and huge from the black chill, becoming pale and glimmering, becoming Luise rising in her vast and ivory nakedness in the dark, in the night sea. So deep, the sea! So vast and comfortless! I shaded my eyes with my hand and looked down into the transparency of the gin in my glass, smooth brightness in the shining dawn and Luise seen across the water rising naked, huge, gleaming in the shining dawn.

'Are you looking into the past?' said Melanie.

'It's looking into me,' I said, with Luise again at Mr Chow eleven years ago. You're everything I've ever wanted in a woman.

'Istvan's told me about you and Luise. What is it with you and him and women? Does he break them in for you or what?'

66

'This is only the second time it's happened.'
'It hasn't happened yet.'
'Maybe I'll get lucky.'
'Here's to luck,' she said.

11 The Big Rain

Blue-black shiningness, bluish-white shining on the puddles on the football pitch in the rainy night all starred with lamps and windows. Always in November there comes such a night, blue-black and shining and wild with rain and wind and brown leaves blowing. In the morning suddenly the plane trees on the far side of the common are bare winter trees.

Windowed shapes of light on the ceiling, Melanie Falsepercy asleep beside me, Luise rising in the shining dawn in the wild and rainy night.

In the dimness and the shadows of the room I breathed the novembery fragrance of Melanie Falsepercy. Uncovering her I ran my hand down the long smoothness of her back to the roundness of her buttocks. High, high over us there thundered aeroplanes into Heathrow, safe arrivals for the moment; rumbling through the rain the District Line trains took their golden windows homeward in the night, unseen faces mortal and alone.

I went down to the kitchen and opened the fridge. There were three cans of beer, most of a salami, a mouldering of old cheeses, half a tub of margarine, half a jar of marmalade, half a pint of milk and the head of Orpheus.

'Loss!' it said. 'That's what she was to me, you know: she was the loss of her even when she was apparently the finding of her, the having of her. And I was the same to her, I was to her the loss of me. We were the two parts of a complementarity of loss, and that being so the loss was already an actuality in our finding of each other. From the moment that I first tasted the honey of Eurydice I tasted also the honey of the loss of her. What am I if not the quintessential, the brute artist? Is not all art a celebration of loss? From the very first moment that beauty appears to us it is passing, passing, not to be held.'

'Please,' I said, 'can't we talk about beginnings? A beginning is always a new chance.'

'You can jump into a river but that's not the beginning of the river,' said the head.

'Last time', I said, 'you told me that Eurydice said, "Be the world-child with me."'

'You say, "Eurydice said", but I didn't know her as Eurydice at the time and she didn't know me as Orpheus. She said, "Be the world-child with me but you mustn't tell me your name and I won't tell you mine."

'"Why not?" I said to her.

'"The stories are always waiting," she said, "always listening for names; when they hear the names they're listening for they swallow the people up."

'"What stories?" I said to her. "Do you mean oracles and prophecies?"

'"Not oracles or prophecies," she said, "nothing declaimed by priestesses or seers. I mean the stories no one knows about or warns us of – they're waiting to happen, they crouch like hungry beasts impatient for their day."

'"You think there's a story listening for our names?" I said.

'"Hush," she said, "don't let it hear us talking. Be the world-child with me and love me nameless, thou given of the goddess." Her breath was sweet, I kissed her again. "Why do you taste of honey," I said.

'"Perhaps I'm the queen of the bees," she said.

'"And am I the drone that dies in the nuptial flight?" I said.

'"You will be king of the bees," she said, "and it will be the queen that dies of loving." And she was like a queen then, strong and eager as she clasped me to her, this world-child woman in whom I entered the mother-darkness and the mystery. I felt myself becoming story and I was afraid.'

'But you were the world-child with Eurydice.'

'The world-child whose innocence holds the world together? Yes, in that first golden afternoon I was.'

'What about the rest of the time you and Eurydice were together?'

'For a while I was, then I wasn't. Were you?'

'Only for a while.'

'I have in mind a little terracotta figure I have seen,' said the head, 'a little terracotta dancer from Taranto – the motion of her and the swing of her draperies in the dance passing, passing into stillness. Let us say that I put into your hands this little terracotta dancer, and the beauty and the tragedy of it become the whole world to you, become all that is precious and to be enshrined in your heart, take on even a magical significance so that you know in your heart that if ever this little dancer is broken then the world is lost. And in you a devil stirs, a devil with a hammer in its hand.'

'And yet,' I said, 'people *do* love each other and live out their lives together.'

'How do they do it?'

'I don't know, but they do.'

'Have you done it?'

'Not yet.'

'Have you tried?'

'More than once.'

'Tell me about the last time.'

'Her name was Luise.'

'Tell me about Luise. What was the idea of her?'

'What an odd question.'

'It came to me', said the head, 'that when people fall in love they entrust to each other the idea of themselves.'

'Do you mean their own idea of themselves?'

'I mean the essential idea of them that perhaps they don't even know themselves. Each holds out to the other this obscure and unknown thing for the other to perceive and keep safe. What was the idea of Luise?'

'You keep saying "was" as if she's dead.'

'I say "was" because I'm speaking of the time when she loved you. What was the idea of her?'

'Fidelity.'

'Fidelity,' said the head. 'Did you know that when she was with you or is it only now that you know it?'

'Only now.'

'How is it that you know it now?'

'Why do you have to ask so many questions? What good can it do either of us?'

'What is fidelity to you?'

'Fidelity is a matter of perception,' I said. 'Nobody is unfaithful to the sea or to mountains or to death: once recognized they fill the heart. In love or in terror or in loathing one responds to them with the true self; fidelity is not an act of the will: the soul is compelled by recognitions. Anyone who loves, anyone who perceives the other person fully can only be faithful, can never be unfaithful to the sea and the mountains and the death in that person, so pitiful and heroic is it to be a human being.'

'I don't think that's true,' said the head; 'I don't think it has anything to do with perception – I think some people are faithful by nature and others are not. Do you think Luise perceived you fully?'

'No.'

'And was she faithful?'

'Yes, she was faithful to herself, faithful to anything she put her hand to, and faithful to me.'

'As far as you know.'

'I think it would have been beneath her dignity to deceive me; she was very dignified.'

'Eurydice was a big perceiver,' said the head, 'she was constantly perceiving, her perceptions gave her no rest. My singing terrified her – I don't mean little ordinary songs like the ones I did before I met her, I mean the kind of singing that I began to do on that golden afternoon. She heard in it the death of the tortoise, the death of the world-child, and the end of our love.'

'How did you do that singing?'

'Something would get me started, maybe a dragonfly or the light on the river or the look of a tree at night. I'd feel the ache in my throat just before the song came and my throat would open in a particular way as if I were an instrument shaped by the song that used me. When I heard the sound of the lyre I was again the tortoise and again there came the pains of death, the colours and the blackness. People said they heard more than one voice when I sang – they heard a strange human voice and they heard a second voice not human, voice of darkness, voice of

> moment under moment, world under
> world, dark under dark . . .'

The voice of the head of Orpheus changed, became estranged from itself, descanted above itself as it spoke more and more rapidly, the words blurring together as in an auctioneer's chant or the muttered praying of a fanatic:

'voice of the olive tree itself and notself, singing sunlight, singing shadow, singing greenlit shade and moonwind . . .'

The two voices became more and more separate, the upper one seeming to speak faster than the lower; it sounded as if the voice of the mind was hurrying above the slow and ancient animal self:

'singing dark, dark, darkness
down, down, down . . .'

The words faded into silence, then the head said in its normal voice, 'Of course when I sang there was the music of it.'

'And that was the singing that moved stones and trees and charmed wild beasts?'

'I don't think it actually *moved* stones and trees; what it did was put them in a new place for those who heard the singing. Animals were entranced by it. Eurydice hated it, she said that music was never meant to do what my singing did.'

'Did others like it? Did a lot of people come to hear you?'

'Yes, a great many people came, some just because they liked to be in crowds, some for the singing and some for the freak show — many times after the singing I had convulsions and bled from the nose and mouth.'

'Did you want to sing like that?'

'Wanting doesn't come into it, I am that which responds.'

'I think of you and Eurydice,' I said, 'and I wonder what the idea of the two of you is.'

'I think of that constantly,' said the head. 'Over and over again I live that golden afternoon by the river when my song brought the strange and many colours of death into her dream.'

'And yet,' I said, 'it was as if she'd been waiting for that song, as if the death in it awakened the life in her — she too is that which responds.'

Just then I heard Melanie's bare feet on the floor behind me and I closed the fridge as she came into the kitchen. She was wearing my anorak for a dressing-gown and she looked wonderfully naked in it.

'Anything good in there?' she said.

'Three cans of beer, most of a salami, a mouldering of old cheeses, half a tub of margarine, half a jar of marmalade, half a pint of milk, and the head of Orpheus.'

'Let's have a look at the head of Orpheus.'

I opened the fridge.

'Oh my God,' she said.

'What do you see?'

'It's all right, it's only a rather filthy old cabbage but I must be very suggestible because just for a moment I could've sworn I saw this dreadful-looking head with no eyes and the flesh all eaten away.'

'Yes,' I said, 'it's a dreadful-looking thing.' The head of Orpheus went on being itself but it kept its mouth shut as I carried it into the hall and put it in the larder under the stairs.

'It *was* the head of Orpheus before it turned into a cabbage, wasn't it?' she said. 'For you, I mean.'

'Yes, it was, and please don't tell me what Tycho Fremdorf did with *his* head of Orpheus in the film.'

'He didn't do anything with it; he simply watched it go by as it swam upriver. Then he said, "Behind the front of the day the head of Orpheus swims unseen." The subtitle was "NARDIM DEMSTRA VAJ ONDRA TSINTA ORFNANDO ULZVANJO."'

'Then it never told its story?'

'No, it never spoke, it only uttered a strange unearthly melancholy cry. Istvan did it on the Fairlight; he used the cry of the great northern diver and that sound the rails make in the underground when a train's coming.'

'Wheats-yew, wheats-yew?'

'That's it; and then the rumble and clacking of the train.'

'But the head never actually spoke.'

'Not a word.'

'It spoke to me.'

'Well, it isn't a competition, is it.'

'I don't know what it is but I'm trying not to lose.'

'What did it say to you?'

'We talked about Orpheus and Eurydice and that sort of thing.'

'You still want Luise back, don't you?'

73

'How'd we get from Orpheus and Eurydice to Luise and me?'

'You've just answered my question.'

'No, I haven't. Luise's part of the past – it's just that I've been finding it difficult to work my way into the present.'

'What about what happened earlier this evening? Was that what you call working your way into the present?'

'That wasn't work.'

'I hope not. What are you going to do with that cabbage?'

'I don't know. Maybe I don't have to think about it just now.'

'Maybe after I leave it'll be the head of Orpheus again.'

'I can't say what it'll do, we haven't known each other that long.'

'You and the cabbage or you and I?'

'The head of Orpheus and I.'

'I shouldn't like to come between you.'

'I think we're all in this together, you and I and the head of Orpheus.'

'In what?'

I was about to say, 'This story,' then I decided not to. 'I don't know.'

'For a moment I thought you were going to say, "This story." I'm glad you didn't.'

'So am I.'

12   In the Morning

In the morning I came awake as I always do, like a man trapped
in a car going over a cliff. Melanie stirred, clinging to the sleep
that was casting her off. I looked at the long line of her back,
the sweet Velasquez curve of her hip, then I got up and parted
the curtains to see under a dark sky the distant red and green
lights of the District Line and the long grey curve of iron
sweeping towards Fulham Broadway. It was Saturday; an idle
train stood empty while from behind it a Tower Hill train slid
majestically round the long and shining curve.

I went to the larder under the stairs and found the head
weeping quietly. 'What is it?' I said. 'What are you crying
about?'

No answer except a quiet snuffling.

'Oh, for God's sake,' I said, 'if you're going to carry on like
that at least tell me what's on your mind.'

Still no answer. I heard Melanie in the kitchen. 'I'll talk to
you later,' I said to the head.

Melanie was naked under my anorak again, smooth and
sleepwarm as we kissed good morning. I was looking forward
to a slow and easy weekend together but in a few minutes she
was dressed, had toast and coffee, and gathered herself for
departure. 'Sol's going to drop off a typescript at my place,' she
said. 'I'll phone you later.'

When she'd gone I went to the larder to talk to the head but
found only an exhausted-looking cabbage. 'Once begun, the
story must be finished,' I said, 'remember?'

Nothing. I put it in a carrier bag, took it to the river,
dropped it in, came home and sat down at my desk and
typed:

IN THE MORNING
In the morning I came awake as I always do, like a man
trapped in a car going over a cliff. Millicent stirred . . .

No, Millicent wasn't right.

75

trapped in a car going over a cliff. Monica stirred . . .

Definitely not Monica, women named Monica have never fancied me.

In the morning I came awake as I always do, like a man trapped in a car going over a cliff. Melissa stirred, clinging to the sleep that was casting her off.

Page one? I didn't think so. Suddenly the idea of turning one's experience into a story seemed not only bizarre but perverted; the idea of such a thing as page one seemed at the very least a monstrous vanity. Where was the beginning of anything, how could I draw a line through endless cause and effect and say, 'Here is page one'? Well of course either one was a storyteller or one wasn't, and it looked as if I wasn't – all I could do was describe phenomena as I experienced them. I looked at the two sentences on my page one attempt until the telephone rang and it was Melanie.

'There went today and tomorrow,' she said. 'Sol's given me a twelve-hundred-page first novel by the ex-mistress of General Sphincter to read and I've got to give him my report on Monday.'

'Twelve hundred pages! What size?'

'A4.'

'Good job they're not foolscap. Why don't you do it here? It'll be really cosy.'

'No, I've got to be in my own place with my own space-time. I'll ring you Monday.'

Well, I thought as I hung up, there you have it: you need her more than she needs you.

The telephone rang again and Sol Mazzaroth jumped out of it and grabbed me. 'How's it going?' he said.

'GNGGX. NNZVNGGGG. NNVLL.'

'Terrific. When can I see it?'

'FNURRN.'

'Great. Any time after three.' He shook my hand and climbed back into the telephone as the dusk wrapped itself around me like a python.

Evening shadows make me blue, I thought in the voice of Connie Francis, *when each weary day is through. How I long to be with you, my happiness.* The dusk continued both as python and ambience as it filled the room with what the dusk brings, roads and faces long gone, action not to be revoked, the past that is always now and

THE LITTLE TRIBUNAL OF THE DUSK

Shadows, shadows, voices from otherwhen, faces from time lost, said the dusk. Do you remember the maze near Bicester and whom you walked it with? Do you remember the Cairn o'Mount Road over the Grampians, the tawny owl in the grey afternoon? And Portknockie? Do you remember the boat in the rain? Do you remember St-Paul-de-Vence and Kensington Square? Do you remember the olive tree? Do you remember, do you remember?

Yes, I said, I remember everything because this is

THE DUSK VS ME

How do you find? said the dusk.

Guilty, I said.

The universe, hissed the dusk as python, as ambience, as tribunal, is a continually fluctuating event that configures itself to whatever is perceived as centre.

I turned to the Vermeer girl, I looked at the colour plates in the books and the big print over the fireplace. She wasn't there, the virtue had gone out of my poor copies, they were empty of her. The room filled up with a desolation that drained the virtue out of everything. All of the colour and accumulated detail of books and pictures, posters, puppets and art objects, charts and maps and Chinese kites, all the comradely clutter of shortwave radio and tape recorders, computer and printer, all the things on my desk, the stones from places of power, shrivelled oak leaves and dry acorns from favouring trees, shells from memory's store of sunlit ocean (some of them broken and revealing mystical helices), the little china cat that played with a golden ball, the pensive bisque mermaid from a forgotten aquarium (Luise had given me both of those), the sombre broken-nosed painted lion (relic of some cast-iron peaceable kingdom) – everything in the room, the colour and pattern of Oriental carpets and cushions and furniture until now harmoniously sharing territories of light and

77

shadow – all of it stopped looking right and began to look wrong.

It was after closing time. From the footpath along the common came shouts and drunken singing where jackals and hyenas prowled the wastes and the satyr cried to his fellows. This was only Saturday night; there was still Sunday to get through.

In the morning as always the *Sunday Times* and the *Observer* slid through the letterbox and flopped grunting to the floor, their review sections and supplements heavy with news of Juan de Fulmé, Boumboume Letunga, Jarvis Bendable, Charmian Rox, and every other writer who was not Herman Orff. I got through the day by answering letters and paying bills, my regular Sunday refuge.

In the evening I looked for the Vermeer girl again in the print over the fireplace and in the books and again she wasn't there. 'Why aren't you there?' I said to her. 'What have I done to make you go away? Where have you gone?'

No answer.

'You've always been here,' I said. 'How am I supposed to get along without you?'

Still no answer.

'Listen,' I said to the radio, 'give me her voice at least.' It was tuned to 7320 kHz, in the twittering and tweetling of the vast hollow aerial miles a soprano was singing *Tales from the Vienna Woods* in Russian. Desolate, those woods. Radio Moscow began to fade, and scarcely had I touched the tuning dial when a new voice came in, a girlish voice as fresh and clear as the run of spring water over clean stones. It was a presenter I hadn't heard before, reading the news on Radio Tirana's German transmission on 7310 kHz. I was caught by her brilliant simplicity; her speech was wholly unmannered, wholly uncovered, it came out of her with her breath and there was in it a fragrance as of her breath and an incandescent eroticism. She read the news like a schoolgirl standing up straight with her feet together, her voice dancing a little with the enjoyment of its own physicality.

She spoke of *Amerikanischer Imperialismus* enchantingly and unmaliciously, and she finished each news item with a rising inflection in which one could hear her tidy small pleasure. Her voice made in the crackling and whispering of the evening airwaves a quiet place of its own. Knowing hardly any German I was able to let go of all comprehension so that she came to my ear naked, giving me, unvitiated by any surface meaning, the sound that signified only herself. Whenever she paused for breath I was shocked by the intimacy of it. It was just such a voice as the Vermeer girl might have spoken with.

Still listening to her I put on a videotape of a Channel 4 film of a tidal mangrove forest in Borneo and the crabs with bodies like human faces. I ran it with the sound off. The moon rose over the sea and the voice of the girl from Tirana moved with the spring tide that flooded the mangroves as the great female crab silently exploded her fertility into the sea, clouds of infant ancient faces rising around her. The German faded out, the sweet voice was itself only, beckoning wordlessly in the moving waters under the moon.

'What?' I said. 'What are you saying?'

Come and find me, said the Vermeer girl.

13　The Hague

Liverpool Street at night is a darkling place; it darkles. Out of the dimness stare the red and yellow illuminated signs of the JAZZ BUFFET AND BAR, of CIGARETTES AND SWEETS. In the dimness under the fluorescent lights at the ticket barriers travellers manifest themselves halfway between chiaroscuro and silhouette. There is a general echoing of rattling and rumbling, there is a dark and stertorous clamour. The Harwich train will leave at 1940 from Platform 9.

I'd gone to Orpheus Travel in the Fulham Road but it was shut down; BILL STICKERS WILL BE PROSECUTED, said a sign on the window. Behind the window there were only scattered papers on a dusty floor. I bought my ticket at Thomas Cook in Harrods.

As the train pulled out I was astonished to see how many illuminated clockfaces looked out of the station into the night. I didn't count them; I was strongly satisfied by them, that in the hurrying past of the uncelebrated moment these heralds were yet present to trumpet silently with their luminous faces all departures, all arrivals.

The train wheels, now authorized to take up their song of distance, clacked and clattered their traditional shanty of miles. The unseen boat not yet arrived at, the dark sea waiting, these already lent significance to the travellers on our train; everyone looked interesting.

An ordinary mirror is silvered at the back but the window of a night train has darkness behind the glass. My face and the faces of other travellers were now mirrored on this darkness in a succession of stillnesses. Consider this, said the darkness: any motion at any speed is a succession of stillnesses; any section through an action will show just such a plane of stillness as this dark window in which your seeking face is mirrored. And in each plane of stillness is the moment of clarity that makes you responsible for what you do.

Consider this, said the train wheels, repeating the message

tirelessly moment after moment on the miles of cold iron that lay shining in the dark that led to Harwich and repeating face on face the faces reflected in the windows. Harwich achieved, the windows became empty of faces.

Signs pointed to LADIES, GENTLEMEN, SHIPS. My passport was stamped; with the other seagoers I went up an escalator and along a glassed-in passageway from which we could see the hinged shell of the stern of the *Prinses Beatrix* lifted to receive a stream of cars.

Having climbed the gangway and been directed by stewards to our cabins we then moved haltingly on such stairways as offered until the number on a door matched the number on a piece of paper in one's hand. People stood in little knots of bafflement, then disappeared.

In a little while I reappeared in the self-service restaurant, sitting at a table with my notebook, a ham sandwich, and a bottle of beer. An illuminated clock on the quayside looked in through the glassed-in side of the restaurant. The glass was steamed up and dropleted, and on this misty surface appeared a show of moving quayside shadows as the ship cast off its moorings and eased out into the North Sea. In the bright light of the restaurant people ate and drank as the geometric shadows stroked past on the whiteness of the foggy glass.

The whiteness and the shadows withdrew from the glass as the *Prinses Beatrix* moved out. Night showed itself above the receding quayside and its many clustered bluish-white lights. Between us and those lights appeared a widening watershine. Bluish-white and yellow lights slid rearward; cranes and gantries, booms and cables and other marine articulations offered their detail growing smaller, smaller.

Actually, said the bluish-white lights, said the yellow, there is no place whatever, no place at all. We have told you this before in topographies of emptiness and on the roads of night, you have known it looking out of strange windows. You have always known it.

No, I said, I don't know that. I'm not ready to know that. I have always found place, I have always had places. Death as it follows me takes away one place after another; sometimes it's like the breaking of a string of beads; the beads all rattle on the floor, some roll into dark corners. But my places are not yet all gone.

Night and distance occupied the ship, hummed in the hollowness of it, throbbed in the engines of it, drove it like a line across a screen. I wondered if the Kraken felt the tremor of it, wondered if the blind and questing head of Orpheus swam before it, cleaving the darkness ahead of the bow wave and the marbling white wake that widened and vanished in the night. Certainly this night passage sang in the olive tree.

The train for Amsterdam, chic in yellow paint with blue blazons, stood ready just outside the customs hall. With other travellers I got into it and looked out of the window at a dark tower that lifted its head above some trees and showed an illuminated clockface. On the window that I looked through there was, instead of a crossed-out cigarette, a crossed-out bottle. What a good idea to cross things out on windows, I thought. What a convenience.

The sky as it grew lighter showed itself to be a good firm northern before-dawn sky. A resigned-looking man opposite me, very small, very moon-faced and eastern, put a black-cased radio-cassette recorder carefully between his legs like a shrine, extended the antenna, put on headphones, and sank back into the whispering of the news in his head.

The carriage filled up with people, rucksacks, and suitcases; the train stood motionless; it was not due to move for another hour. The sky grew more and more pale and more and more by-the-sea. There were dark blue streaks in it now and a few scattered marine-looking clouds. Across this paling sky flew the black shapes of silent gulls. Over the electric railway stretched a precision of gantries and wires. Between the train and the dark tower of the clock there was lifted up the black shape of a hammer-headed crane. It swung round and moved out of sight. A white light appeared above the trees. From the head of the moon-faced eastern-looking man issued tiny compressed Mozart. The sky was now dove-grey and altogether marine in its character.

At 0730 the train moved. We passed bulldozers and tractor shovels impassively moving earth, we passed cattle standing in

82

quiet pastures while the mists of dawn rose round them. We passed sheep, blocks of flats, canals with perfect little bridges, and black ducks on silver water. There was no darkness to mirror our faces; our eyes looking out saw such world as framed itself in the windows with the crossed-out bottles.

In due course the train arrived at the beautiful Pieter de Hooch-looking red-brick station in The Hague. According to my books the Vermeer girl was at the Mauritshuis, but when I bought a map the newsagent told me that the Mauritshuis was closed for renovation and the paintings were to be seen at the Johan de Witthuis, which he marked for me.

A little after nine o'clock I arrived at the Johan de Witthuis, which did not open until ten o'clock. By that time I was longing for the conveniences as well as for the Vermeer girl. There were no signs anywhere that said anything like HERREN, no bifurcated pictographs. Until ten o'clock I walked up and down looking at shop windows and wondering whether a preoccupation with dikes had made the Dutch constipated.

When the doors opened I paid my admission and bought an illustrated catalogue on the cover of which was Vermeer's *View of Delft*. I said to the man at the desk, 'Are all the paintings from the Mauritshuis here?'

'No, only the ones in the catalogue.'

'But the Vermeer, the *Head of a Young Girl*, that's here, isn't it?'

'No, the only Vermeer is this one.' He indicated the reproduction on the cover of the catalogue.

'Where's the *Head of a Young Girl*?'

'It's on loan in America.'

'Thank you.' Pondering the complexity of this demonstration I went inside and made my way to the *toiletten* in the basement.

When I came back up the stairs I went into Zaal A where I found myself looking at two panels attached to each other, Nos 843a and 843b, a diptych, evidently, by G. David (1460–1523). Two narrow vertical panels offering a dark wood, many leaves, a stream, a donkey, a bird, two oxen, a road, a stone building with a tower or a silo. A mill? Unlikely. The word hospice came into my mind. Did the stream flow under an arch and into the building? Or did the road glitter, did the road flicker and shine

83

not like a road? The dancing beast of the mystery, was it in this mystic wood? What a dark whispering in those many leaves! Come and find me, she had said. In this dark and whispering wood?

It occurred to me then that this Witthuis, this new abode, was a place that the Vermeer girl had physically departed from. She'd gone away over the water. Out of her Witts? Away from wittingness, perhaps; beyond the reach of intellect. Her old dwelling-place had been the Mauritshuis. I had no Dutch dictionary but I had my pocket German Langenscheidt with me so I looked to see if there was anything close to Maurits in German. *Maurer* was bricklayer, mason. The number of the railway carriage in which I had travelled here from the Hook of Holland had been 727. G is the seventh letter of the alphabet, B the second. GBG: GIRL BECOMES GONE. The Vermeer girl had moved from the house of bricks, of gross earthy matter, to the house of wits, of the mind, but intellect proving barren she had become gone while Hermes for a joke sent me to find her. No, it wasn't just Hermes – she herself had told me to come and find her and in some way not yet revealed to me this was the place where she would be found, I could feel it.

I looked in my catalogue to see what it had to say about this dark wood painted by G. David. There was no mention of it whatever. I went to the man at the desk. 'Those two panels by David,' I said, '843a and 843b, they're not in the catalogue.'

'No,' he said, shaking his head, 'they're not. They're in the catalogue that's in the shop.'

'Where's the shop?'

'Through there.'

I went to the shop and bought the *Mauritshuis Illustrated General Catalogue* and a postcard of the Vermeer girl. Two French schoolgirls were buying the same postcard. 'But where is this painting?' one of them asked the man at the counter. 'We can't find it.'

'It's in America.'

'When does it return?'

'Next year.'

Turning in the catalogue to David, No. 843, I read:

David, Gerard
Born ca 1460 in Oudewater, died 1523 in Bruges. Worked
in Bruges, where he was the most important artist after the
death of Memling.
Two forest scenes
P. each 90 × 30·5. The versos of the wings of a triptych;
the left one with a donkey, the right one with two oxen. Ox
and donkey recur in the middle panel. The latter, depict-
ing the Adoration of the child and the rectos of the wings
are in the Metropolitan Museum in New York.

I went back to Zaal A and stared at the two panels. A space
suggested itself between them and I waited to see what would
appear in the space.

Someone was looking over my shoulder. I turned and saw a
tall thin man with a large light-bulb-shaped bald head and
those drooping oldtime-gunfighter moustaches much favoured
by American television actors. From the hang of his face
however I guessed him to be European, possibly Scandinavian.
He seemed to be drawing himself up into his head preparatory
to speaking, and as I was the only other person in the room I
waited to hear what he would say.

'Rectos no,' he said. 'Mmnvs? Everything is metaphor and
metaphor is the only actuality. Here we have the versos of the
wings of a triptych, here we have only the other sides of the
missing rectos that when folded shut covered the Adoration of
the child. Mmnvs. Nnvsnu rrndu.'

'Did I understand you to say nnvsnu rrndu?' I said.

'Mmnvs.'

'You're thinking of existing?'

His head seemed to grow larger and balder and more
light-bulb-shaped. 'You observe me, sir,' he said. 'You observe
me consistently and three-dimensionally manifesting, with
aplomb, myself both as picture and sound. Do you not?'

'I do.'

'I revert to the tremendour of this metaphor, the other-
sideness of versos without rectos and the child gone missing,
out of our sight, offering only its rejection of our potential
adoration.'

'"Tremendour." I haven't heard that before.'

'Tsrungh. From its otherness of place it speaks the encrustation, the palimpsest, the ultimate dialectic of what Redon called "the deep health of the black". This is where I get my jollies; I am a creature of the deeps.'

'Says who?'

'Says *Sight and Sound* for one. They did an eight-page piece about my work: "The Unslumbering Kraken".'

'I've stopped reading *Sight and Sound*, I don't think film people should be allowed near words, it's bad for everybody.'

'I agree completely. I speak only in pictures. With me the image is everything, carrying within it as it does the proto-image, the after-image, and the anti-image. This is why here I have come to speak to the Vermeer girl and to hear what she will say to me but alas, she is gone over the water and here I stand looking at this enchanted wood with its missing rectos and its centre that could not be held. This utters to me most powerfully.'

'What did you want with the Vermeer girl?'

'I'm in love with her. She is that aspect of the Mother Goddess that dominates my being, my perception, my innermost and uttermost blackness, my seminal vesicles. She is the proto-image of the femaleness of things; always have I spoken to her in the whispering of the night, in that warm and creatureful darkness where the flickering of the here-and-gone shows its little uncertain flame.'

'Have you no shame? How can you say such things in a public place to someone you've never seen before? You don't even know my name.'

'That signifies not at all; you know *my* name.'

'No I don't.'

'I've told you it: Kraken, Gösta Kraken as you know very well. Not for one moment do I believe that you've stopped reading *Sight and Sound*. From the faltering cadence of your stare I perceive that you recognize me from those many photographs of me in that publication and elsewhere. Fnss. The self-consuming antistrophe of your silence tells me that you resent my head of Orpheus swimming up the Thames.'

'Faltering cadence of my stare! I'm not taking that from you, nor "self-consuming antistrophe" either. Don't you come the deconstructionist with me, you ponce. I've never even seen your swimming head of Orpheus.'

'Very well then, tell me your name. I can see that you will be fractally asymptotic in your resonances until we have spoken this out.'

'My name is Herman Orff and you've never heard of me.'

'Oh, but I have. Luise has mentioned you several times.'

There was an upholstered bench behind me. I sat down on it.'

'Luise', I said, 'has mentioned.'

'You. More than several times, reverberantly and with plangency.'

'What is Luise to you?'

'Lost. Gone. Two years only, then Znrvv! No more Luise. A note on the kitchen table like an unaccompanied cello in a studio with dusty windows.'

'Don't roll the credits over it; just tell me plangently when she left you.'

'Seven years ago, with my sound man.'

'What do you suppose she heard in him?'

'Other music.'

'And what did she ever see in you?'

'Flickering images.'

'Of what?'

'It doesn't matter, it's the flickering that gives the excitement. Being is not a steady state but an occulting one: we are all of us a succession of stillnesses blurring into motion with the revolving of the wheel of action, and it is in those spaces of black between the pictures that we experience the heart of the mystery in which we are never allowed to rest. The flickering of a film interrupts the intolerable continuity of apparent world; subliminally it gives us those in-between spaces of black that we crave. The eye is hungry for this; eagerly it collaborates with the unwinding strip of celluloid that shows it twenty-four pictures per second, making real by an act of retinal retention the here-and-gone, the continual disappearing in which the lovers kiss, the shots are fired, the horses gallop, rrks?'

'Luise saw all that in you, did she?'

'It isn't only that I make films, I am in myself a big flickerer and women respond to this. I'm so much there/not there/there/

not there. Very exciting. It stimulates a woman's natural holding-on reflex.'

'And yet Luise seems to have let go of you.'

'Nothing is for ever.'

'Fallok composes electronic music; I write novels; you direct films; the one after you (whom she probably left five years ago) was a sound engineer. Before Fallok she was with a man who ran a restaurant.'

'By now it's a computer programmer or a doctor; into the arts she came and out of the arts she has gone, vnnvvzzz. What did we do wrong?'

'You don't know? You don't know what you did wrong?'

'My behaviour was impeccable. When she was with me she moved among top-class people – film stars, composers, painters, writers; we went to all the best restaurants, we had friends with yachts and villas on the Côte d'Azur and in the Greek islands: the whole thing was conducted in the style one would expect of me.'

'Were you faithful to her?'

'Faithful!' His large face leapt back as if I had hit him with a pizza. 'Faithful! I can only be faithful to the flickering; more than that I don't accept the moral authority of.'

'Two years with you. I can't understand it. I'm rotten but you're a real creep.'

'Were you faithful to her?'

'No.'

'Then why do you look at me as if you've just come down from the mountain with stone tablets in your hands?'

'Because I know I'm rotten and you don't know that you are.'

'You make a virtue of necessity; being a self-confessed rotten you are aware of your rottenness. Being unrotten I have not such an awareness.'

'Why don't you flicker off and manifest your sound and picture somewhere else.'

'You're a very troubled person, znnzz?'

'I can live with it.'

'Are you certain of that?'

'Don't let me keep you; you must have many urgent demands on your time.'

'I assure you that only a charitable impulse has kept me in your company this long; ordinarily I don't like to get too close to obscurity, it's like quicksand.'

'You'd better back off then before you get swallowed up.'

'Are you working on a novel now?'

'Yes. Why?'

'Good luck with it, I hope you resolve your difficulties.'

'What makes you think I'm having difficulties?'

'You seem to be falling into the spaces between the successive appearances of yourself. If you're not careful you'll disappear.'

'If I stop thinking you it might well be you that disappears.'

'I'm disappearing now,' he said, 'but you will continue to think of me,' and he withdrew.

Thinking of him I went upstairs and stood in front of a painting by Frans Post (1612–80), Catalogue No. 915, *Gezicht op het Eiland Tamaraca*. It was a strange painting, a little on the naif side – as apparently artless in its composition as a snapshot, as if the painter had sat himself down on the beach, aimed himself at the island across the water, and painted whatever came between him and it: two black men; two white men; two horses; an expanse of pinky dawn-looking water; two small boats moored by the island; in the foliage of the island was a naked place that looked bitten out by a giant. One of the black men balanced a basket on his head with one hand. He wore nothing but a pair of short white trousers. The other black man, also in white shorts, had put down his basket of yellow fruit and stood holding the reins of a white horse. One of the burdensomely clothed white men stood on the beach waving at or pointing towards the island while the other sat his chestnut horse which had a white blaze on its face and a white sock on the offside hind leg. He did not look at the island.

Perhaps the actual time in the painting was not dawn. But here in the Johan de Witthuis the water across which the Island Tamaraca was seen was dawn water. I could feel in this dawn a presence looking out at me, I could feel in it the buzzing and the swarming of what was gathering itself. I could feel myself approaching the correct frequency, I held myself carefully tuned to it when it came.

Out of the pinky dawn water, naked and shining in the

dawn, rose Luise, quivering like a mirage between the beach and the island seen across the water. Quivering, shimmering, her body becoming, becoming, becoming a face loosely grinning, with hissing snakes writhing round it in the shining dawn. Around me ceased the sounds of the day; the stone of me cracked and I came out of myself quite clean, like a snake out of an egg, nothing obscuring my sight or my hearing. The Gorgon's head, the face of Medusa, shimmered luminous in a silence that crackled with its brilliance. Her mouth was moving.

What? I said. What are you saying?

You have found me, she said. I trust you with the idea of me.

You, I said.

Yes and yes and yes and yes, she said. Look and know me. Hold the idea of me in you by night and by day, never lose it.

Yes and yes and yes and yes, I said, I look and I know you. I will hold the idea of you in me by night and by day, I will never lose it.

She was gone in the pinky dawn water between the beach and the Island Tamaraca.

I went out of the Johan de Witthuis and looked all around at the unimpeachable objectivity of the Dutch daylight. One would be ashamed to draw badly in that light.

Moving carefully so as not to disturb the unknown idea I had lunch in some sunny windowed place that looked out on the street. Then I walked back to the station, noticed a little hotel opposite with its name in quotation marks, '*Du Commerce*', took a room for the hours remaining until the departure of the boat train at 2200, was shown upstairs, lay down, fell asleep, and dreamed of a secret cave behind a waterfall.

It was between four and five in the afternoon when I woke up. Careful not to ask myself any questions, I had a shower, went down to the bar, drank beer, drank gin, brought a second beer up to my room and looked out of the window at the early evening. The light had gone a grainy purple-blue. Beyond the station stood white office blocks, fluorescent-lit against the sky, looking as if they belonged to memory and time long past. Yes, I thought, there were people then; they too were happy and sad, they too looked out upon just such a purple-blue evening. Through the glass sides of the Pieter de Hooch railway station I saw the yellow carriages slide in and out.

I switched on the overhead room light, it was a little flame-shaped bulb in an electrified oil-lamp. Somewhere such bulbs are manufactured; what does it say on the box? 10 W ETERNA-FLAME DEPRESSION perhaps. Outside the window a double street lamp stood up like a luminous pinky-orange hibiscus. Beyond the lamps the yellow trains arrived and departed with a soft and rapid dinging of bells in the grainy purple-blue evening. Passing under my window was Luise walking slowly away towards the station in a yellow mac the same colour as the trains.

I ran down the stairs and out into the road. She was still there, manifesting herself as ordinary reality and not disappearing. She paused at the sound of my footsteps and turned. 'Herman,' she said. 'What are you doing here?'

'I came to see the Vermeer girl but she's gone to America. What about you?'

'I'm here with my husband, he's installing a computer system.'

Time ceased to be an automatic progression: the present moment exploded into millions of sharp-edged fragments and nothing followed. The bells dinged softly, the yellow trains moved in and out, the purple-blue darkened but the next moment did not come. It seemed so little to ask, that the next moment should come. Perhaps if I moved my mouth. I moved my mouth, it said, 'You're married then, you finally found the right one.'

'Yes, I found the right one.'

I had a piece of folded-up paper in my pocket, I always do: yellow A4. 'Luise,' I said, giving her the paper and a pen, 'please write your name and the date on this for me.'

'Why?'

'Because all of a sudden it'll be some other time and I want to have something from this time.'

She wrote her name and the date, the piece of paper is stuck on the edge of the monitor screen along with the Vermeer-girl postcard. I was right, all of a sudden it was some other time and the engines of the *St Nicholas* were throbbing as they drew a line across the night from Hook of Holland to Harwich. In my

91

hand were the postcard and the folded yellow paper on which was written *Luise Nilsen* and the date. She lived in Oslo now, her husband's name was Lars, he was forty-two, tall and bearded, they did a lot of skiing, they did a lot of sailing, they owned a forty-foot ketch named *Eurydike*, they had a daughter named Ursula who was almost a year old, they called her Ursel, Luise thought of me sometimes, she'd read *Slope of Hell* and *World of Shadows* and recognized herself and incidents from our two years together, that time seemed very far away now. We sat in the bar at the '*Du Commerce*' and talked as if it was a possible thing to do: there she was, I could have reached out and touched her, and she was gone out of my life for ever. I had no part in her days and nights, she would continue without me as if I were dead.

I went out on deck and walked aft to look at the white wake widening astern in the night. Seeing the actuality of Luise married and gone for ever, was that what the stone had cracked and freed me for? I could feel that something had happened, I could feel the Hermes of it, could feel myself on a night road to somewhere else. One couldn't ask more than that — to be sometimes on a night road to somewhere else. 'I have no name but the one you give me,' I said, 'no face but the one you see.'

Cleaving the foam like a periscope was a telephone in which crouched the telephonist Lucretia, bellowing above the sound of the engines and the hiss of the sea along the ship's sides that she had a call for me from Sol Mazzaroth.

14   No Balls

Ring, ring, said the telephone when I got home.

'Hello,' I said.

'Herman Orff?' said Lucretia, flicking her whip against her boot.

'Yes.'

'I have a call for you from Sol Mazzaroth.'

'Thank you.'

A little advance silence came out of the telephone like ground meat out of a meat-grinder. I wrapped it neatly in white paper and tied it with string.

'Herman?' said the voice of Sol Mazzaroth.

'That's me.'

Sol's hands came out of the telephone and rubbed themselves together briskly. I offered them the neatly wrapped silence.

'Herman,' said Sol, 'tomorrow's the editorial meeting for Vol. One, Number One. Where are we with Orpheus?'

I saw my current account rolling its eyes like a steer in the slaughterhouse. If you had balls you wouldn't be a steer, I said as I lifted the hammer.

Look who's talking, said the current account. If you had balls I'd have been dead long ago. Go on, kill me, let's see you do it.

I put down the hammer. Maybe we can work something out, I said. After all, they're even doing Shakespeare in comics nowadays. And I'm sure it's what Shakespeare would've wanted, he was a popular writer in his time.

Shakespeare was what he was and you're what you are, said the current account: you're a miserable no-talent coward.

One day you're going to push me too far, I said.

That'll be the day, it said.

'Herman?' said Sol. 'Are you there?'

'Sol, I haven't been able to get started on Orpheus yet.'

'Herman, what are you telling me? Just the other day you

93

said, – hang on, I've got it right here – you said, "GNGGX."
You said, "NNZVNGGGG," you said, "NNVLL." And you said
you'd have something for me to look at on FNURRN, which is
today in case you hadn't noticed.'

'Sol, there's a lot more to this Orpheus thing than you might
think.'

'Please, spare me the song and dance. When can you have
something for me?'

'Can I ring you up tonight?'

'I'll ring you. Tell me when.'

'Late. Round about midnight.'

'Right, talk to you then.'

What I like about you, said the current account, is that
you're reliable. You can always be relied on to have no balls.

I'm not sure what I'm going to do, I said. I've got to think
about it.

Right, said the current account. We'll talk again soon, OK?
We'll have lunch.

I rang up Istvan Fallok. 'I've just come back from The
Hague,' I said. 'I ran into Luise there.'

'Luise! What's she doing?'

'She's married, big bearded husband named Lars. They go
skiing and they have a forty-foot ketch, it's called *Eurydike*.
They have a year-old daughter named Ursula. They live in
Oslo and Lars installs computer systems. How's that grab you.'

'You needed me to know about it, right?'

'Right.'

'OK, I know about it. Bye-bye.'

'Wait. Did you know about Luise and Kraken?'

'Yes, I knew about that. Bye-bye again.'

I sat there with the telephone in my hand thinking of
Melanie. No, I thought, wait a little.

I put on the tape of the Blue Note Thelonious Monk Volume
One that begins with 'Round about Midnight'. Beyond my
window the grey wind rattled the brown leaves and two boys
ran past kicking a football that thumped and skittered among
the parked cars. Sheltered in Monk's midnight dome, his caves
of nice, I typed on to the screen:

THE STORY OF ORPHEUS

94

Something hit the front door with a sodden smack. I opened it and the head of Orpheus leaped up and fastened its teeth in my arm. Filthy and battered, its features flattened as if it had been rolling through the streets for years, it hummed and buzzed its blind rage.

'Nice to see you again,' I said. 'To what do I owe the pleasure of your company?'

The head continued biting. Blood was running down my arm.

'Something's bothering you, isn't it,' I said. 'Is it anything I've done?'

The head jerked itself towards the monitor and THE STORY OF ORPHEUS.

'Is that it?' I said.

The head nodded.

'I've told you that Sol Mazzaroth wanted something in the Orpheus line,' I said. 'I was about to see what I could do with it.'

The head shifted its jaws and got a better bite.

'You'd rather I didn't. That's a bit dog-in-the-manger, isn't it? You won't finish your version and you don't want me to make up my own.'

The head opened its mouth to speak and I caught it as it fell. 'You keep making me appear,' it said, 'and I'm so tired.'

'*You're* tired? What about me? Life wasn't hard enough so I had to go to The Hague and find Luise with a big bearded husband and a daughter and a forty-foot ketch.'

'Wide Justice,' said the head.

'What do you mean, "Wide Justice"?'

'That's what the Greek name Eurydike means.'

'I can handle Wide Justice; it's the forty-foot ketch that gets up my nose. I can see the husband all bearded and fearless at the helm, his name is Lars. The boat's name is *Eurydike*.'

'Bastard.'

'Indeed. I travelled over land and sea to find the Vermeer girl and what did I get for my trouble? Bearded Larses and forty-foot ketches and Gösta Kraken.'

'Who's Gösta Kraken?'

'He's one of the Luise old boys. He did a film called *Codename Orpheus*.'

95

'Ponce. Who's the Vermeer girl?'

I told the head about the Vermeer girl.

'She's another Eurydice,' said the head.

'What else is new?'

'You can't go looking for Eurydice.'

'Look who's talking.'

'My perceptions and my understanding change from moment to moment,' said the head. 'What I mean is that you don't find Eurydice by looking for her.'

'I found the Vermeer girl gone,' I said. 'I found a dark wood, I found the Island Tamaraca, I found Medusa. And I found Luise definitively gone. Standing before me and gone for ever.'

'You found Medusa?'

'Shimmering and luminous above the pinky dawn water.'

'I never found Medusa,' said the head.

'Were you looking for her?'

'Every man is, I know that now. Do you know what the idea of her is?'

'No.'

'Behind Medusa lie wisdom and the dark womb hidden like a secret cave behind a waterfall. Behind Medusa lies Eurydice unlost.'

'Let it be, you're wording it to death.'

'Perhaps you don't need me any more,' said the head, as my arms began to feel leaden.

'Don't be offended, please, we still have the story to finish.'

'I wonder if I can sing now.'

'Please don't. When you tried to sing that first morning by the river the silence was awful, I don't want to hear it again.'

'Don't be so delicate. As long as I have any kind of being I have to keep trying.'

'Surely there's a time for singing and a time for silence.'

'My business is singing, not discretion. Be quiet and listen. What time of day is it now?'

'Afternoon. Hang on, if you're going to sing I might as well record it this time.' I put the head on my desk and plugged a microphone into the tape deck.

'I'll sing an evening song,' said the head. Just as the mouth opened an aeroplane passed overhead. The lips and tongue moved but again I heard nothing. I touched the head but wasn't sure whether I felt any vibration or not. After the plane had gone the mouth continued to move in silence for quite a long time, then it closed. There was a little pause, then the head said, 'Well?'

'I didn't hear anything, although it's hard to be sure, there was so much noise from the aeroplane.'

There was a boy's face at the window. His hand appeared, pointing at the head of Orpheus on my desk. I went to the front door and found two boys on the steps. 'Can we have our football back?' said the first one. 'We didn't mean to kick it at your door.'

'I haven't got your football.'

'Yes you have. You picked it up and took it inside and it's on your desk now. We've been ringing your bell for a long time.'

'The bell's disconnected.'

'We've been knocking as well,' said the second boy.

'I never heard it.'

'Well, anyhow, give us back our ball,' said the first boy.

'What did your ball cost you?'

The first boy looked at the second boy. 'Ten quid.'

'There's a sports shop in the Broadway near the bus stop; you can buy another ball there, OK?' I gave him ten pounds and both boys disappeared.

'Where were we?' I said to the head.

'I've sung for you twice,' it said, 'and both times you've said you haven't heard me.'

'This time the microphone was listening too; let's see whether it heard anything.' I rewound the tape, put on headphones, and played it back. It was surprising at first to hear the head speaking in my voice but there was of course nothing extraordinary in it; if it could use a football for manifesting itself there was no reason why it shouldn't use my voice to speak with. When it said on the tape that it was going to sing I turned up the volume and watched the level meters. There went the aeroplane. The cooling fan of the Apple II was audible, and above it there was a faint high-pitched humming that went up and down in a halting and uncertain tune that was just loud enough to move the luminous bars on the level meters a stroke or two past the -20 decibel mark. Faint and distant it struggled to reach me like some broken melody coming round

97

the ionosphere through the storms and surges of the shortwave night to my lost outpost in Fulham. It was of course my own voice but I hadn't remembered humming at the time; it sounded as if I might have been trying to follow something that I was straining to hear.

'Well?' said the head. 'Can you hear yourself hearing me?'

'Yes, but why can't I hear *your* voice, the voice of Orpheus singing?'

'Let's be realistic; I'm a hallucination.'

'Right, that's why the tape recorder hears only my voice. But if I hallucinate an Orpheus voice when you talk to me why can't I do it when you sing?'

'Maybe I'm not real enough to you.'

'Maybe nothing is. Maybe the third novel isn't real enough to me, maybe Luise wasn't real enough to me.'

'Maybe you yourself aren't real enough to you.'

'How does the world-child do it? How does the world-child hold the world together and keep it real?'

'The world-child has been told that this is a world,' said the head, 'and it believes it; it is the energy of this belief that binds the world together. The world-child holds in its mind the idea of every single thing: root and stone, tree and mountain, river and ocean and every living thing. The world-child holds in its mind the idea of woman and man, the idea of love.'

'Who told the world-child all this that it now believes?'

'Each thing told itself to the world-child: the tree; the mountain; the ocean; the woman; the man. You and I, we have told ourselves to it.'

'And the idea of love? Who told that to the world-child?'

'It didn't have to be told,' said the head. 'This idea arises of itself from that energy of belief that keeps the mountains from exploding and the seas from going up in steam. It's only a kind of cohesion that binds together possibilities that have spun together out of the blackness.'

'Like you and Eurydice.'

'It didn't hold us together long.'

'Why not?'

'Even the beginning wasn't very auspicious, was it,' said the head. 'The first I ever heard of Eurydice was the sound of her weeping.'

'That was because she dreamed she was the world-child and she was afraid; that was nothing to do with you.'

'Yes, it was,' said the head. 'She was weeping because she knew that the world-child is always betrayed.'

'And that was in your song?'

'Of course it was; it was in the strange and many colours of the death of love.'

'Her weeping came before your singing,' I said. 'Maybe those strange and many colours in your song came from the weeping that started you singing.'

'Obviously.'

'What's so obvious about it?'

'Don't you understand?' said the head. 'There's only one.'

'Only one what?'

'Only one femaleness, whether it's called Eurydice or Medusa or Persephone or Luise. As Eurydice/Persephone she opened underworld for me, the world under the world, the moment under the moment. And from underworld came my song of love's beginning and the betraying of the world-child and the death of love that made her weep.'

'Oh God,' I said, 'it just keeps going round in a circle.'

'She never liked my singing,' said the head, 'I've told you that. Once she took the lyre out of my hands and said, "Love is its own music." But that doesn't really mean anything, does it? I mean, if music is what you do then that's what you'll do, isn't it. Then she said to me, "You emptied the tortoise-shell for your music and now you're emptying us."'

'Maybe it wasn't only the music that was bothering her.'

'You're thinking of other women.'

'Yes.'

'I remember how their eyes shone in the firelight,' said the head, 'and beyond the firelight the wild beasts crouched and black trees nodded in the night. I remember the dawns when I found myself in strange places encircled by trees and stones and sleeping figures wet with dew. I remember the tops of the trees swaying in the dawn wind, how the night was still in them like a cat biting the neck of its mate.'

'Groupies.'

'I never said I was any better than anyone else,' said the head.

99

'And yet,' I said, 'I suppose the world-child is greedy for sweets as all children are.'

'No, it isn't. The world-child perceives the lover as the whole world, the world-child is greedy for the sea and the mountains and the death that live in that one person who is loved.'

'I told you the first time we spoke', I said, 'that your morality might be too much for me.'

'It's too much for me as well,' said the head. 'My perceptions have always been beyond my capabilities.'

'Then you accept that this world-child is some kind of an impossible ideal.'

'Whatever it is,' said the head, 'it's an idea that won't let go of me.'

'But you weren't able to go on being the world-child,' I said. 'You lost it, and now you roam the world rotting and eyeless, telling your story to strangers like a drunk in a bar. Is this your punishment?'

'Being Orpheus was my punishment.'

'For what?' I said.

'For killing the tortoise.'

'Can that one killing matter so much?'

'Nothing matters more than anything else. Things arrange themselves in certain ways and it is left to us to make the connections.'

'And what's the connection between you and me? I know you're the first of my line and all that but why are you telling me your story?'

'I am that which responds,' said the head, 'I've told you that. You said yes three times and I was compelled to tell my story.'

'Before I said yes three times you asked me three times if I wanted to hear the story.'

'Well, it's a story that wants to be told, isn't it.'

'And you made me take it on me that the story would be finished,' I said. 'Why did you do that?'

'The story is different every time,' said the head, 'and every time there are difficulties – I always need help with it and I'm always afraid it won't go all the way to the end.'

'Different each time. How can that be?'

'How can it not be? A story is a thing that changes as it finds new perceptions, new ideas.'

'Fallok was trying to do it with music,' I said. 'How far did he get?'

'Not very.'

'What do you think my chances are?'

'I don't know,' said the head, 'but if you can't do it there'll be somebody else.'

'You mean if *we* can't do it.'

'Yes of course. Didn't I say we?'

'No, you didn't. Why do you have to keep going through the story over and over?'

'It's got to come out differently one day,' said the head.

I looked away for a moment. When I looked back the head had become a football, one of those plastic ones they sell at Woolworth's for three or four pounds.

'Well, Herman,' said Sol Mazzaroth, 'here it is round about midnight.' He hadn't bothered to ring, he just jumped out of the telephone wearing red silk pyjamas and a black silk dressing-gown with a gold monogram and was pacing backwards and forwards through the clutter on my desk. 'How're we doing?' he said. Pretending not to hear I stuffed him back into the receiver and took the phone off the hook.

Hello, said my current account. I was just passing by and I thought I'd look in. You keeping well? Everything all right?

You said I had no balls, I said.

You know I was just kidding around, said the current account. I didn't mean anything by it. What are you doing, where are you going?

But I'd already jumped into the telephone and hurled myself through the circuits to Sol Mazzaroth asleep in his red silk pyjamas which were monogrammed the same as his dressing-gown. I shook him roughly, averting my eyes discreetly from whoever else was in the bed.

'Herman!' he said. 'What time is it?'

'Three o'clock in the morning.'

'What's happening?'

'I'm not going to do it.'

'Why not?'

'Orpheus wouldn't like it.'

101

'Herman, with respect, Orpheus was a wonderful musician but I doubt that he knew anything about magazine publishing. Stay with it and I'll talk to you a little later in the morning, OK?'

'Sol, I'm sorry but it's not on. I really am not going to do it.'

'Herman, you say you can't do it but you still haven't given me a reason I can understand.'

'I can't do it because it's got to come out differently one day.'

'That doesn't make sense.'

'It does to me.' Through the dark and murmuring circuits I made my way back to my place. The current account lay dead on the floor, a thin trickle of blood coming from its mouth. From over the mantel the Vermeer girl smiled down on me.

Herman, she said, you're a hell of a guy.

15   Life after Death?

I went to bed and the next thing I knew I was awake again and it
was getting on for ten o'clock in the morning. Ring, ring, said
the telephone, ring ring. Seize him.

'I'm right here,' I said. 'I'm tired of running. Here I stand.'

'I have a call for you from Sol Mazzaroth,' said Lucretia.

'Yes,' I said, 'bring forth Mazzaroth in his season.'

Sol stepped out of the telephone and looked at me in
disbelief. 'Herman,' he said, 'was it a bad dream or did you
actually phone me at three o'clock this morning and say you
couldn't do it?'

'Yes, it was a bad dream and that's what I said.'

'But why, Herman? Surely you've done tougher adaptations
for me: look at *War and Peace*, how you got through it in
twenty-five pages, I still tell people about that.'

'I know, Sol. This is just one of those times when something
that was whatever it was becomes something else and all of a
sudden it's too much.'

'Herman, when I think of what we've been through together
since the old Hermes Foot Powder days I can't believe this is
happening. Together we built *Classic Comics* and made it a
beacon of literacy at newsagents everywhere. John Buchan,
Dostoevsky, Victor Hugo – you name it, we put it in speech
balloons.'

'Believe me, Sol, I'm grateful for everything you've done for
me. If it weren't for you I'd still have to bath and shave and go
to an office every morning if I could find an office to go to.'

'And you're going to throw it all away.'

'You know how it is,' I said. 'There comes a time when a
road comes to an end and you have to say, "This is the end of
the road."'

'But it's not the end of our friendship,' he said.

'Of course not.' We both looked at our watches.

'Well, it's going to be a more hectic day than usual. Take
care, Herman.'

'You too, Sol,' I said as he climbed back into the phone and was gone.

So here we are then, I thought. This is the first day of the rest of my life. I got dressed, had breakfast, hurried to my desk. The corpse of the current account was half-buried under discarded pages. I uncovered it, went through its pockets and found enough to live on for six months if I managed very carefully.

'All right,' I said, 'let's get organized.' My voice was frightening in the silence. I switched on the radio and got the Voice of Greece with male and female singers one after another singing songs with 'S'agapo' in the refrain. All of them sang the words soothingly, almost lullabyingly. *S'agapo, s'agapo.* I love you, I love you.

'All right,' I said again. The football was still on my desk. I took it to the usual place near Putney Bridge and dropped it into the river.

When I got back I sat down and typed on to the screen:

1 LOOK FOR FREELANCE COMIC WORK.
2 TRY TO FINISH ORPHEUS STORY WHEN HEAD TURNS UP AGAIN.
3 NO MORE OTHER PEOPLE'S ORPHEUS.

Ring, ring, said the telephone.

'Hello,' I said.

'Hello,' said a vigorous female voice, 'this is Hilary Forthryte, I'm with Mythos Films. I hope you don't mind my ringing you up out of the blue like this.'

'Not at all.'

'Can you talk for a moment or are you in full spate?'

'Not yet, I'm a late spater.'

'Ah! I know what you mean. What I'm phoning about is to ask you whether you might like to do a film with us. We've got Channel 4 funding for six one-hour films under the series title *The Tale Retold*; we'll be doing new versions of old myths and legends with six different directors. The first one I've spoken to is Gösta Kraken and he said he wants to work with you and a composer called Istvan Fallok.'

There was a pause at my end.

'Do you know Kraken well?'

'No. I've only met him once.'

'But you're familiar with his work.'

104

'I've heard about *Codename Orpheus*.'

'But you haven't seen it?'

'No, I haven't.'

'We've got a print of it, I can arrange a screening any time you like. What's interesting is his use of Orpheus as semiosis rather than as story.'

'Ah.'

'We've also got prints of *Bogs* and *Quicksand* – those were the last two before *Codename Orpheus* and you can see his obsessions developing, his preoccupation with wetness and ooze as primal mindscape and his vision of a discarded world. Anyhow, without committing yourself at this point, do you think you like the idea in principle?'

'Have you got a subject in mind for our film?'

'Eurydice and Orpheus.'

'But he's already had a shot at that.'

'As I've said, he's obsessive. He says it's an inexhaustible theme and he's got a lot of new ideas for another approach.'

'What sort of money are we approaching it with?'

'We've got a budget of £250,000 per film; that works out at £8,000 each for director, composer, and writer, plus residuals. That's not a lot of money but you'd be completely free to do what you like and I should think it might be quite fun if you've got the time to take it on.'

'All of us getting paid the same, I'm surprised that Kraken agreed to that.'

'He looks on this as a necessary exploration and he's particularly keen on an equal partnership with no ego trips. I thought perhaps the four of us could meet for lunch. Would Thursday be all right for you, one o'clock at L'Escargot?'

'That sounds fine.'

'Perhaps you'd like to see *Bogs* and *Quicksand* and *Codename Orpheus* first.'

'I'll just have a look at *Bogs* to begin with, I'll save the others for later.'

Forthryte arranged a screening of *Bogs* at Mythos for the next day, Saturday. I rang up Melanie to ask her along.

'Where've you been?' she said. 'I've been phoning you for days.'

Oh yes, I said in my mind. Did you phone me on Monday as

you said you would? Did you phone on Tuesday? 'I went to The Hague,' I said. 'I'll tell you about it when I see you. Would you like to see *Bogs* with me tomorrow?'

'The Kraken film? Yes, please.'

16 Blvgsvo

The plain white gothic capitals on the flickering black said:

BOGS
BLVGSVO

'What language is that?' I said to Melanie.

'He makes it up,' she said. 'He likes the effect of subtitles. In his book, *The Flickering*, he says that under our ordinary speech there are always invisible subtitles in an unknown tongue. In all of his films since 1975 the actors speak in English and the subtitles are in Krakenspeak.'

There was music, something rather like the Bach B Minor Mass played backwards, as words appeared on the screen:

Between the dead city and the threshing floors lay the bogland.

NIM VUGMIS NIM DENGSVO ZOKNIS NA BLVGSVODMA.

Squelching and sucking sounds were heard and from a very low angle we saw, black against a dark sky, bulky figures in wellingtons crossing a boggy landscape:

Three times daily came the messengers.

TIMTAM TOM RIG SHOLDIK.

Over the music there came snippets of voices speaking in several languages at irregular intervals as the scene cross-dissolved to two bearded men, well wrapped up, inside a very dark hut:

One day . . .

TOMZO . . .

'I'm going to the bogs,' said the man on the left.

VLAJO BLVGSVO.

'Why?' said the one on the right.

ZOM?

'Why not?' said the one on the left.

DOMZOM?

The two men stared hard at each other and cross-dissolved to a bog under a dark sky. The camera moved in to look at some water. Under the water was a woman in a wedding dress. Her mouth moved as the water became ice. She seemed to be saying, 'Never.' There was no subtitle.

'Did she say "Never"?' I said to Melanie.

Melanie nodded.

A man sat by a blackboard with his head in his hands. 'There is only one quintessential image,' he said.

ZVEM NULZI LODZA NURVURLI

A little boy appeared and opened a newspaper-wrapped parcel to show a small severed hand. 'Look what they gave me,' he said to the camera.

NAL ZAL RIN DOMZI

A flight of white pigeons filled the dark sky as the camera tilted down to their reflection in the water which was no longer frozen.

'The blackness is the ultimate dialectic,' said the bearded man who had been on the left in the hut. He was sitting in the water.

LEVSNOK FURMIL SNEV.

'I think I want to go now,' I said.

'I'll see you later then,' said Melanie. 'I want to see the whole film.'

I sneaked out of the building without meeting anyone – the place was mostly empty – came out into the thin wintry sunlight of Wardour Street and went home.

The film had started around two o'clock in the afternoon. I was expecting Melanie by five or six at the latest but she didn't turn up till well after eight.

'I thought I'd get here sooner,' she said, 'but Gösta Kraken turned up at Mythos and we went for drinks after the screening.'

'Good,' I said. 'Did he show you his ultimate dialectic?'

'Ah. Here we go.'

'No, there you went.'

'That sounds rather final.'

'There you went for drinks.'

'Yes, there I went for drinks, I do that sometimes, I'm a drinkivorous person. Why'd you walk out of *Bogs* anyhow?'

'I find that I don't want to be with Gösta Kraken's mind all that much.'

'That's going to be a problem if you're working on a film with him, isn't it?'

'Maybe I can live with it. I need the money.'

'Are you sure it's his mind that's bothering you?'

'What do you mean?'

'I mean him and Luise.'

'He's told you about that, has he.'

'Yes, he has. It seems to have a mystical significance for him, as if it's created a metaphysical bond between you and him and Istvan.'

'Feels more like bondage.'

'Maybe bondage is what you really like. You seem to enjoy harnessing yourself with regrets and chaining yourself to the past.'

'I'm not even sure there is a past,' I said. 'My life is littered with old action like empty beer cans but it's all in the present.'

'Let's get some full beer cans and some fish and chips,' she said.

We went to a place near her flat in the North End Road. The fluorescent lighting and the white tiling amplified the roads and voices in my mind while asseverating the particularity of this only, this distinct and unmerged moment. I noticed again Melanie's eyes as they had looked the first time I saw her, open wide, with white showing all round the pupils. Clip-clop, her little black boots had gone in the shady grove of her sudden woodland. She had just said something.

'What did you say?' I said.

'I said that fish and chip shops are metaphysical.'

'Everything is.'

We took the fish and chips and beer up to her flat near the West Kensington underground station. The room that over-looked the street was large and uncluttered; the walls and ceiling were white, the overhead light was an orange paper globe; there were blue drapes on the wide window; there were a drawing table with a typewriter and an Anglepoise lamp on it, a blue wooden chair, two red filing cabinets, and some unpainted bookshelves in which among the books and typescripts were a tape deck, amplifier, tuner, turntable and speakers. There was a large print of Rousseau's *Sleeping Gipsy*. Under the desert moon the gipsy woman slept, the lion watched, the stillness waited. In the background a green river and a range of mountains.

I wondered what was moving at this moment in Gerard David's mystic wood at the Johan de Witthuis, I wondered what was rising from the pinky dawn water between the beach and the Island Tamaraca. I'd told Melanie about everything but Medusa. ·

Looking at the *Sleeping Gipsy*, I said, 'What do you think is going to happen in that picture?'

'First tell me what you think.'

'I think the gipsy is in a dream. The lion isn't in the dream so the gipsy is safe for the moment. But if the gipsy wakes up or the lion falls asleep there could be big trouble.'

'You'll notice', said Melanie, 'that the gipsy's got a lute or a mandolin.'

'Yes, I notice that.'

'Well, this gipsy's been busking around for a while and she's tired of doing it alone. Her birth sign is Leo so she's put an ad in *Time Out*: "MUSICAL LEO SEEKS PARTNER." The lion answered and they've arranged to meet by the river but he's late and she's fallen asleep waiting for him.'

'The question is', I said, 'has he got any talent?'

'If not he can always get by on his looks,' she said.

We ate our fish and chips and drank our beer contentedly; our windows were golden in the night. From the front window I looked down on the Saturday night North End Road and saw Gom Yawncher go unsteadily past with a bottle in his hand. He was singing:

> Yessir, I can boogie
> but I need that certain song –
> I can boogie, boogie-woogie
> all night long.

Yes, I thought, maybe I've got that certain song now. She was so beautiful, there was in the air such bright promise of nights following nights. I walked around the room taking in the herness of it, looking at book titles, picking up small objects. On the drawing table next to the typewriter was an A4 folder. *Eurydice and Orpheus*, it said.

'Eurydice and Orpheus!' I said.

'Yes. I'd rather you didn't look at it.'

'You're writing something.'

'Yes.'

'For yourself? Off your own bat?'

'For *Classique*. It's the one Sol wanted you to do and you turned down.'

'He didn't waste any time, did he,' I said.

'There's no mandatory waiting period before someone else has a go, is there? Especially as you'd already wasted whatever time there was to waste.'

'Sol told me to give it my best upmarket thinking. Are you thinking upmarket?'

'For four thousand quid I'll think however he likes. It's a commercial proposition.'

'And you're a commercial person?' As I said that I told myself there was no reason why Sol shouldn't offer her the same money he'd offered me; looking at it with strict objectivity and grinding my teeth a little I accepted that all those years of speech-ballooning hadn't made me worth any more than the rankest beginner. And the novels, after all, counted for nothing.

'I'm no more commercial than you are,' she said. 'I'm just doing what you've been doing with your comic-writing all these years – I'm buying time.'

'You're working on a novel.'

'Don't worry, it isn't catching.'

'What do you mean by that?'

'Well, you recoiled so violently that I thought I'd better reassure you.'

'Reassure me that there's no danger of my writing a novel.'

'That isn't what I meant but if that's how you choose to take it then all right.'

'Sorry,' I said, 'I'm being stupid.'

'You said it, I didn't,' she said.

'I wonder if we could possibly wind back the evening to where we were just before I saw that *Eurydice and Orpheus* folder?'

'I don't know,' she said. 'Now the gipsy's wondering whether the lion really is a lion or maybe just two very small blokes in a lion suit.'

111

'Two very small blokes,' I said to my face in the mirror as I brushed my teeth alone at home, 'and no boogie-woogie for either of them.'

17 Where Do We Go from Here?

'Veuve Clicquot,' said Hilary Forthryte to the waiter. She was
a vivid-looking woman with long dark hair and she was
wearing a Ralph Lauren safari outfit with very expensive
boots. Sitting next to her was a small gimlet-eyed bearded man
in a leather jacket. 'My partner Ivor Dreft,' she said. 'We
thought it might be a good idea for him to be in at the
beginning of this.'

The skylight in the top-floor dining-room of L'Escargot let
in a better class of daylight than was available in the street; the
people in the room all looked as if they were in full colour in a
Sunday supplement. Youth and beauty, talent and fame were
all around me.

'Hilary!' said an immense bearded man, also in safari
clothes. He kissed Forthryte on the mouth and during the kiss
they both said, 'Umm-mmhh!' When they'd done that he
made signs of professional recognition to Kraken, Fallok, and
Dreft and nodded pleasantly to me. You may be nobody, said
his look, but you might have money or influence and what does
it cost me to nod pleasantly. 'Are we going to see you on
Sunday?' he said to Forthryte.

'I wouldn't miss it,' she said, and immediately I imagined a
great coruscation of youth and beauty, talent and fame. 'Ferdy
Phyvemill,' she said, 'Herman Orff.'

'Hi,' said Phyvemill, getting the better grip and crunching
my hand.

'I've got your *Lost Incas of the City* on tape,' I said. 'I've
watched it four times so far.'

'Piracy,' said Phyvemill. 'Send me money. Are you in the
business?'

'Herman's working on a Channel 4 film with us,' said
Forthryte while I manifested humility.

'Doing what?' said Phyvemill.

'Speech balloons,' I said.

'Herman's a writer,' said Forthryte.

113

Phyvemill withdrew his earlier pleasant nod. 'Watch him,' he said to Kraken, made his farewells, and hulked off.

'His last picture was a disaster,' said Kraken.

'It grossed $50 million last year,' said Dreft.

'Plus it came top at Cannes and kept a lot of people in work for almost two years,' said Forthryte.

'Most of them were shooting documentaries on Ferdy Phyvemill at work on his film,' said Kraken.

'Was that *The Secret History of the Mongols*?' I said.

'More like the secret history of the Brits,' said Fallok. 'The only Mongols were the extras, the horses, and the porters.'

'Here's to Eurydice and Orpheus,' said Forthryte as the waiter filled our glasses.

'It's entirely correct that you should name them in that order,' said Kraken, 'Eurydice being the whole of which Orpheus is the part.'

'Would you say that she's the sea in which the blind and voyaging head of Orpheus swims?' I said.

Everybody looked at me with a strange look.

'I have said precisely that,' said Kraken, 'in that scene in *Codename Orpheus* in which Eurydice is the sea that Orpheus swims in. Is it possible that you have forgotten that image and the sound of her singing?'

'Actually I haven't seen the film,' I said.

'Why not?' said Kraken.

'I haven't wanted to know any modern versions of the story,' I said. 'I like my ideas to come to me out of ignorance.'

'And what ideas have come to you out of your ignorance so far?' said Kraken. 'How do you propose to take hold of our theme?'

At that moment the waiter appeared with our starters. I'd ordered grapefruit but I found on my plate the sliced-off top of the head of Orpheus. It was inverted like a bowl from which I was about to spoon up the brain.

'Excuse me,' I said to Kraken and the others. I quickly wrapped the half-head of Orpheus in a napkin and made for the stairs.

'Is everything all right, sir?' said our waiter as I almost knocked him down.

'It's perfectly lodza nurvurli,' I said, 'thank you.'

'I DON'T WANT TO BE HERE!' shouted the brain of Orpheus.

'Be quiet!' I said, 'I'm getting you out as fast as I can.'

An elderly woman whom I recognized as a dancing girl from an early James Bond film smiled brilliantly at me as I stood aside to let her pass me on the stairs. 'Talking takeaway?' she said.

'It's my fault for ordering something hemispherical,' I said, and she nodded sympathetically.

'EURYDICE! ' shouted the brain. 'THAT WAS EURYDICE, SHE SMELLED SO GOOD!'

'That wasn't Eurydice,' I said. 'Please stop embarrassing me.'

'I WANT TO SMELL HER AGAIN!' shouted the brain.

'Thank you,' I said as someone opened a door for me and someone else opened another door. 'It'll be quiet once I get it outside,' I said.

Once in Greek Street and a little distance from L'Escargot I opened the napkin. 'All right,' I said, 'what've you done with the rest of you?'

'Maybe you're losing me,' said the brain of Orpheus.

'We'll talk about this when we get home,' I said, and found that I wasn't all that keen to get home. I wrapped the brain up again and headed for the Tottenham Court Road tube station. I used the subway on the east side of Charing Cross Road because there are always buskers there and I hadn't yet seen Gom Yawncher busking.

Sure enough, there he was, playing some cheap little plastic Pan-pipes badly and shuffling about in what I supposed was his idea of pre-classical Greek dance.

I dropped 10 p into his cap. 'I'm not surprised to see you here,' I said.

'Thank you, guv, I'm not surprised to see you either.'

'Really,' I said, 'your eagerness to make an appearance and be noticed however briefly is pathetic. Can it possibly matter that much to you to play these tiny scenes and speak your few little lines?'

He stopped playing and shuffling. 'It's like life, isn't it. Little music in the tunnel, few coins in the cap, here and gone, pfftt. What's in the napkin?'

'The brain of Orpheus.'

'Don't try to be too colourful,' he said. 'Don't come the eccentric quite so strong. Just be natural and let it happen.'

'Let's get something straight,' I said. 'I'm not a bit player in *your* story, you're a bit player in *mine*.'

'Oh yes. Says who?'

'This is intolerable. I'm writing all this down, you know.'

'Writing down what we're saying?'

'Writing down whatever happens to me.'

'What for?'

'Trying to get my head around it.'

'*Now* who's pathetic?' He went back to his Pan-pipes and his shuffling.

'What's pathetic about trying to understand what happens to you?'

'It's cowardly, besides which I don't believe you. I bet you're writing it all down trying to make a story out of it, I can tell by the miserable look of you. You're not really living your life – you're pulling the legs and the wings off it one by one. Why don't you take up vagrancy or crime, it's more manly.'

'More manly! And I suppose busking is more manly too, is it?'

'Not half. Here I am for all to see and hear, doing my pitiful little dance and playing my Pan-pipes badly. Poor sod. Give him a bob or two. I am what I am and being it in plain sight, not hiding behind a book or dressing up in clever words. Any further questions?'

'Not today. Perhaps another time.'

'As you like, guv. And remember, don't push it, just let it happen.'

'You run your show and I'll run mine,' I said.

When I got home I opened the napkin and there was the brain of Orpheus, it hadn't changed back to half a grapefruit. 'All right,' I said, 'tell me what's on your half-mind. Where do we go from here?'

'Are you speaking to me?' said the brain.

'Yes, I'm speaking to you.'

'Are you sure you can spare the time? You seem to be so terribly busy, you have so many things to do.'

'I'm not the one who's playing hard to get,' I said. 'I haven't seen you since you were a football.'

116

'I thought you might want a little time for reflection.'

'Reflection is what I haven't got a lot of time for just now. My *Classic Comics* meal ticket is gone and I've got to do something that'll bring in some money.'

'Other people's Orpheus,' said the brain.

'I don't want to do that film,' I said. 'I've already said no to Sol Mazzaroth and his four thousand pounds but it's twice as hard to say no to eight thousand pounds and there's nothing else on the horizon.'

'Is that the story of you then?'

'I hope not. Tell me what happened with you and Eurydice.'

'We are not a whole story, Eurydice and I; we are only fragments of story, and all around us is unknowing.'

When the brain said that I remembered a flight to Zürich, seeing from high in the air the black peaks of the Alps rising from a milky ocean of cloud.

'That's how it is with the story of us,' said the brain, 'black peaks rising from a white obscurity. There are certain patterns, certain arrangements of energy from which events and probabilities emerge but I know nothing for certain. Do you remember Aristaeus?'

'Yes, I do.'

'He watched with wide eyes when I killed the tortoise and dug it out of the shell. He asked my name and he insisted that I was a story. I remember how he wrote my name in the air. I think I see him scratching words on potsherds. I wish I hadn't told him my name. He kept bees, Eurydice kept bees. I think she learned bee-keeping from Aristaeus.'

'Were they lovers before she met you?'

'I don't know,' said the brain. 'I've told you there isn't a whole story. I don't know what's between them in that space between the making of the lyre and my finding of Eurydice by the river. I think of the buzzingness, the swarmingness, the manyness of bees singing the honey of possibility. I see Eurydice sitting among the skeps under the apple trees listening to her bees. She was afraid that our story would find us but she was always listening for it.'

'How can bees tell a story?'

'The bees don't tell a story but in the manyness of their singing there sometimes comes a story to the one who listens.'

117

'The story that Aristaeus was scratching on potsherds?'

'Broken pieces want to come together,' said the brain, 'they want to contain something. I see Aristaeus with his broken bits of fired clay, each one only big enough for a word or two. ORPHEUS, he has written on one piece, THE TORTOISE on another. As soon as these words are put next to each other there want to be more words: THE ROAD; THE RIVER; EURYDICE. Or perhaps EURYDICE is the first word and in the empty space next to it there appears THE TORTOISE. Or first THE TORTOISE, yes of course, THE TORTOISE first because it is the centre of the universe, because it is the world-child; THE TORTOISE first and then EURYDICE who is again the world-child-tortoise, EURYDICE whose loss is the judgment, whose loss is the reckoning and the punishment.

'The judgment, the reckoning, and the punishment.'

'Yes,' said the brain. 'Eurydice is all that one wants to be faithful to and cannot, and the loss of her is the punishment.'

'How did you lose her?'

'I lost her when I stopped perceiving her.'

'I meant how did you lose her physically?'

'She went off to live with Aristaeus.'

'She wasn't bitten by a snake, she didn't go to underworld?'

'Not in this telling of the story; she simply left me and moved in with Aristaeus.'

'Nothing more dramatic than that?'

'Real life is all there is,' said the brain.

'She left you because of your infidelities?'

'I think it was the story that finally did it. When there was love and happiness there was no story, what there was could not be contained by words. With the death of love came the story and the story found words for it.'

'What happened?'

'You remember that she didn't want us to speak our names,' said the brain. 'We'd made up names for ourselves and those were the names we were known by. Then one night we came to a place and people said to me, "Sing about Orpheus and Eurydice."

'"Who are Orpheus and Eurydice?" I said.

'"Lovers in a story," they said. "Eurydice died of a snake-

118

bite and Orpheus went to underworld to bring her back but he turned around to look at her too soon and he lost her."

"'More likely it was someone else he turned around to look at," said Eurydice, "and the only snake was the one between his legs."

"'I don't know that story," I said. I sang about the kingfisher and the river and blood came out of my nose and mouth and I fell down and had convulsions and when I came back to myself they still wanted me to sing about Eurydice and me. We went away from that place and our names filled our minds, it was impossible not to speak them.

"'Orpheus,' she said to me sadly, "now the story has found us, now we have become story and I must leave you."

"'Why?' I said. "Why must you leave me?"

"'Because Eurydice is the one who cannot stay," she said. "Eurydice is the one who is lost to you, the one you will seek for ever and never find again. Eurydice is the one of whom you will say, 'If only I had known what she was to me!'"

"'If only I had known what you were to me!' I said.

"'You did know," she said. "Orpheus always knows and he always does what he does and Eurydice becomes lost to him. That's the story of us and there's nothing to be done about it."

"'Eurydice!' I said. "I'll change and the story will change. I'll be faithful to you and you'll stay with me because you are all the world to me."

"'Underworld as well," she said, "but I can't stay."

"'Eurydice, Eurydice!' I said. "What shall I do without you?"

"'You will sing better than ever," she said. "Art is a celebration of loss, of beauty passing, passing, not to be held. Now that I'm lost you will perceive me fully and you will find me in your song; now that underworld is closed to you the memory of the good dark will be with you always in your song. Now you are empty like the tortoise-shell, like the world-child betrayed, and your song will be filled with what is lost to you.'"

'And did you sing better?' I said to the brain of Orpheus.

'Yes,' said the brain. 'Day followed night and night followed day and everything was empty, there was no world in the world; the river and the sunlight, the kingfisher and the dragonfly, all were grey. I sat in a little room and the shadows

119

moved on the walls. There was an earring that had fallen on the floor; sometimes it lay in sunlight, sometimes in shadow. In the evenings I went out with my lyre and I sang world and underworld and my songs were deeper and stronger than ever before. No longer did I bleed from the nose and mouth, there were no more convulsions, the songs I sang in my misery were easy and the beauty of them broke the heart.'

'And what then?'

'What do you mean, "And what then?" What more do you want?'

'I want the whole story that I took on me to finish, I want the end of it. Did you just go on singing beautiful songs or what?'

'Little by little the beauty went out of them and fewer people wanted to hear them. I ended up singing for coins in taverns as I had done before I became the Orpheus of the stories.'

'How did you die?'

'In a drunken brawl.'

'What about the Thracian women? Didn't the Thracian women kill you?'

'In a manner of speaking. But they did it one at a time.'

'And how did your head get separated from your body?'

'People are strange,' said the brain, 'they'll take a head that was useless to its owner and expect it to answer all their questions. Mine enjoyed a brief vogue as an oracle until somebody kicked it into the sea and the next mode of the idea of me. But as far as I'm concerned the personal story of me came to an end when Eurydice moved in with Aristaeus and both of us were swallowed up by the commonplace.'

'But you sang better than ever before.'

'What remained was less than what was lost,' said the brain.

'What remained became the endlessly voyaging sorrow and astonishment from which I write in those brief moments when I can write,' I said.

'You must do the best you can with what you've got,' said the brain. 'Eurydice is lost to you but Medusa trusts you with the idea of her.'

I went back through my pages to the Johan de Witthuis and the Island Tamaraca:

Out of the pinky dawn water, naked and shining in the dawn, rose Luise, quivering like a mirage between the beach and the island seen across the water. Quivering, shimmering, her body becoming, becoming, becoming a face loosely grinning, with hissing snakes writhing round it in the shining dawn. Around me ceased the sounds of the day; the stone of me cracked and I came out of myself quite clean, like a snake out of an egg, nothing obscuring my sight or my hearing. The Gorgon's head, the face of Medusa, shimmered luminous in a silence that crackled with its brilliance. Her mouth was moving.

What? I said. What are you saying?

You have found me, she said. I trust you with the idea of me.

You, I said.

Yes and yes and yes and yes, she said. Look and know me. Hold the idea of me in you by night and by day, never lose it.

Yes and yes and yes and yes, I said, I look and I know you. I will hold the idea of you in me by night and by day, I will never lose it.

I'd said that I'd never lose the idea of Medusa but I wasn't at all sure that I knew what the idea was. The head had said, 'Behind Medusa lie wisdom and the dark womb hidden like a secret cave behind a waterfall. Behind Medusa lies Eurydice unlost.' 'Let it be,' I'd said, 'you're wording it to death.' It was a mystery and I hadn't wanted it explained to me. Now I needed to know where I was with it.

'Will you excuse me for a moment, please?' I said to the brain.

Kraken, I typed, can you tell me anything about this mystery?

THIS MYSTERY, said the Kraken, SHOWS ITS MEDUSA FACE TO COMPEL RECOGNITION, TO WARN THAT UNDERSTANDING STOPS BEFORE IT AND GOES NO FURTHER. THIS IS THE FACE OF MEDUSA WHO CANNOT BE IGNORED, CANNOT BE INTRUDED UPON, CANNOT BE POSSESSED. YOU HAVE NEVER GIVEN YOURSELF TO THIS ONE WHO WILL NOT GIVE HERSELF TO YOU, YOU HAVE WANTED ONLY THE SWEETNESS OF

121

EURYDICE TO LOVE AND TO BETRAY. THIS IS THE FACE OF
WHAT CANNOT BE BETRAYED. LOVE CAN BE LOST AND
BEAUTY, BUT NOT THIS FACE OF DARKNESS MADE BRIGHT.
THIS IS THE ONE TO WHOM YOU CAN BE FAITHFUL.

Nobody said anything for a while. I went to the kitchen,
made myself a Nescafé, and brought it back to my desk where I
found half a grapefruit sitting on a napkin. That happens to me
often: I'll find an old coffee on the bookshelf or a banana on the
mantelpiece or myself halfway up the ladder to the attic and not
know how the old coffee, the banana, or I arrived at those
places. I went back to the kitchen, got a bowl and spoon, put
the half-grapefruit in the bowl, and ate it.

Ring, ring, said the telephone.

'Well,' I said, 'what is it?'

'Herman,' said Hilary Forthryte, 'are you all right? We were
all wondering why you wrapped your grapefruit in a napkin
and rushed out of the restaurant.'

'*That* grapefruit! Oh my God, I've eaten it.'

'You artists. Look, Herman, we've got to have a little think
session soon to get this Eurydice–Orpheus thing off the
ground. How's next Wednesday for you? Can I pencil you in?'

'GNGG, NDZNX, MMPH,' I said as what felt like an iron fist
pushed heavily against my sternum.

'Friday any better?'

'Can I phone you back later?' I was already sitting so I
thought I'd lie down. There were too many papers, books,
cassettes and floppy disks on the couch so I tried the floor and
was amazed at the amount of dust, fuzz, and crumbs. There
was a coffee about three weeks old under the couch, my
favourite mug, I'd wondered where it had got to.

'Try to make it soon,' she said. 'Everybody's busy and I'm
stuck with organizing the whole thing.'

My left arm was very leaden; the iron fist had gone but now I
seemed to have swallowed an iron box which was stuck in my
chest. 'Yes,' I said, 'I'll make it soon.'

The local surgery was close by so I stood up, walked there
very slowly, told the receptionist about the leaden arm and the
iron box, and took my place in the waiting-room with five
people being patient and seven National-Health-looking fish

122

being aerated by a stream of bubbles. That's how it is, I thought: a little stream of bubbles till the pump shuts down. I picked up a two-year-old copy of *Harpers & Queen* which fell open to a photo of Gösta Kraken and the headline FROM THE DEEPS: KRAKEN RISING. The corners of the iron box sharpened up a little.

Dr Carnevale looked into the room and called my name and I followed him into his office. 'Pains in your chest and left arm?' he said.

'Yes,' I said. 'At first it was like an iron fist but now it's as if I've swallowed an iron box. And my left arm feels leaden.'

'Let's have your shirt off.' He unlimbered his stethoscope. 'I guess by now you've finished the novel you were working on when I saw you last year. Breathe in.'

'No, actually I haven't.'

'Breathe in again. Very stressful occupation, novel-writing, so I'm told. Do you happen to know Rupert Gripwell? Lean forward.'

'No. Is he a novelist?'

'Undertaker. He says they don't last as long as journalists.'

'Undertakers?'

'Novelists.'

'Why is that?' I said, as he took my blood pressure.

'Says they drink alone too much. People drink faster when they drink alone. You drink alone much?'

'Well, I can't be bothered to go looking for people every time I want a drink, can I.'

'I suppose not. I spend a lot of time in the garden. You've got to have some way of unwinding or everything gets to be too much. How's the pain?'

'It's gone.'

'I don't think it's anything more than angina but I'll book you into St Stephen's so they can have a look at you.'

18　Louisa, not Luise

Watchful in her space of light the night sister sits at the edge of the dark ward. At three o'clock in the morning the moments patter like rain on the roof of night; the silence is a road to anywhere.

At the far end of the ward someone cries out, 'Luise!' There is a rush of nurses, a trundling of apparatus; the fluorescent lights flicker on; the curtains around the bed are drawn; the curtains are opened, a man is wheeled away.

The name he cried out must have been *Louisa*, not Luise. Yes, it must have been Louisa. The bed remains empty, the man hasn't come back. What did he look like? I hadn't noticed the occupant of that bed earlier, he must have been in the day room or asleep or hidden behind a newspaper.

He never did come back. Later they cleared away his things, stripped the bed, and put on fresh sheets and pillowcases. I asked the night sister whether he'd had a snake-and-dagger tattoo and the name *Louisa* on his left arm.

'Yes,' she said. 'Did you know him?'

'We chatted sometimes but I never knew his name. Who was he?'

'Gombert Yawncher.'

'Do you know what he did for a living?'

'He was an actor but I don't think he'd been in work for quite a long time. He told me he used to do the voice for the old Pluto Drain Magic ads on TV, the cartoon ones where Pluto hurled himself down the drain like Superman.'

I remembered those ads, they were done before the account came to Slithe & Tovey. Back then their slogan was 'PLUTO GETS THE DIRT UNDER THE DIRT'.

'His heart gave out, didn't it?' I said.

'Yes, it was a coronary thrombosis. He said to me this morning, "It'll be tonight," and I said, "What'll be tonight?" and he just looked at me and said, "I can't remember my lines any more."'

'It could happen to anybody,' I said.

I went to the day room and stood there in the dark at the sliding glass door that opened on to the balcony. From where I was on the fourth floor I could see, beyond the roofs and dormers of the old part of the hospital, the upper parts of houses on the far side of the Fulham Road. The road itself was not to be seen.

Looking towards the unseen road in that three o'clock in the morning of the November night I imagined Orpheus running, running, saying to the night, 'I have no name but the one you give me, no face but the one you see.' Orpheus as athlete, his limbs and motion graceful in the darkness; Orpheus seen from a distance on the dim Fulham Road under cold November lamps, on the dim Thracian road wending into darkness, the dim white of the road that runs behind the eyes to otherwhere. Orpheus running, running night into day, day into the long road, night into the long world's music. I'd never thought of his body before, only the head.

19   Still Three O'Clock in the Morning

It's still three o'clock in the morning, the night sister still in her space of light at the edge of the dark ward, at the edge of underworld. Her face is in shadow, her white cap flickers, becomes a writhing and a hissing silence. She looks up, her shadowy gaze is on me. The silence crackles with its brilliance, her mouth is moving as it moved above the pinky dawn water between the beach and the Island Tamaraca.

'What?' I said. 'What are you saying?'

'We haven't had a ten o'clock urine specimen from you,' she said.

20 The Visit

Melanie came to visit me with a bunch of grapes. 'What brought on the angina?' she said.

'The head of Orpheus turned up as half a grapefruit and in an absent-minded moment I ate it.'

'Perhaps that was your way of recognizing that you don't need it any more.'

'It's the other way round: it doesn't need me any more now that we've finished the story.'

'Well, there you are then; you took it on yourself to finish the story and now you've done it and it's off you. That's more of a reason for *not* getting angina.'

'Yes, but it'll take some getting used to.'

'Do you remember in *The Tempest*,' she said, 'Prospero says, "This thing of darkness I acknowledge mine"?'

'Yes, I do.'

'That's what I think you've been doing; and now that you've acknowledged it you can move on to something else.'

'This thing of darkness is where my writing comes from.'

'You mean your comics?'

'No, I don't mean my comics. *Slope of Hell* and *World of Shadows* weren't comics, were they.'

'No, but they were quite a few years back, weren't they. What's this thing of darkness done for you lately?'

'Today is William Blake's birthday,' I said.

'What's that got to do with it?'

'Nothing. He just came into my mind, that's all. He said that what men and women require of each other are the lineaments of Gratified Desire.'

'There's more than one kind of desire that wants gratification,' she said.

'What kind were you thinking of?'

'The desire to stop mucking about and get on with it. Have you started work on the film?'

'No.'

127

'Are you going to?'

'I don't know.'

'Right. I can see what's coming: after a while you'll leave the phone off the hook and stop answering the door and keep the blinds pulled down and newspapers and letters and bills will pile up in the hall and finally one day they'll break down the door and there won't be anybody there but the thing of darkness.'

'Maybe that's who's been there all along. Gom Yawncher's gone.'

'What do you mean?'

'He was here in this ward and now he's gone, handed in his dinner pail, picked up his cards, hopped the twig, slung his hook, pissed off out of this world.'

'Oh,' she said, and began to cry.

'Sorry, I didn't mean to burden you with it.'

'Yes, you did.'

After a while the grapes were still there but she was gone. Pale wintry Sunday-afternoon sunlight on the grapes.

21   The Seeker from Nexo Vollma

The hospital, having brought me a cup of tea at six o'clock every morning, electrocardiogrammed me, X-rayed me, tested my blood and urine, confirmed Dr Carnevale's diagnosis of angina, advised me to avoid fats and cholesterol and take moderate exercise and lose weight, gave me a little bottle of glyceryl trinitrate tablets, and put me out on the street again. And there I was as before with Hilary Forthryte waiting for my call and the current account dead on the floor.

Quickly I went to the word machine, booted the system master and the word-processing programme, and typed:

Hello, hello. Is anybody there?

WHOM DID YOU WANT?

Well, I thought maybe Medusa.

THIS IS MEDUSA SPEAKING.

Do you remember what you said to me?

WE HAVEN'T HAD A TEN O'CLOCK URINE SPECIMEN FROM YOU.

No, before that, when you spoke above the pinky dawn water between the beach and the Island Tamaraca.

THAT WAS A MYSTERY.

I know, but couldn't we talk about it a little?

NOT NOW.

OK, I said. Sorry I bothered you. I blew some of the dustballs off my desk, emptied the wastebasket, put on a Greek tape, shook some dandruff over the keyboard, stared at the screen, and began to fall asleep. 'No,' I said, 'that's not the way to do it.' I got a videotape from the shelf, it was a BBC documentary about a wedding in Calabria and I was remembering the father of the bride. I ran it fast forward to the part I wanted: there it was just before the end, there was the father, a thin man in shirtsleeves. Setting up his daughter in married life had cost twenty thousand pounds, each of the two families bearing half the cost. This man had used up his savings and borrowed from the bank and he had two more unmarried daughters.

There is music and suddenly he is dancing. His feet move

him in a circle and with his arms and his head he abandons himself; his arms make rhythmic motions of swimming or scattering, his face is rapt, urgent with the marriage of his daughter as his dance carries him around his circle.

I rang up Hilary Forthryte and told her I couldn't do the film, I had too many other things to wind up and I really wasn't going to be free for a new project for a long time. Then I sat down at the keyboard again and looked intently at the screen.

ARE YOU THERE? said the Kraken.

Here I am. What now?

PAY ATTENTION.

I am paying attention.

FAR, FAR DOWN IN THE DEEPEST DEPTHS OF THE HURGO MURMUS LIVES NNVSNU THE TSRUNGH.

Yes, that sounds good. Tell me about Nnvsnu the Tsrungh.

NNVSNU THE TSRUNGH, ALONE IN THE BLACKNESS, THINKING, THINKING IN THE BLACKNESS OF THE ULTIMATE DEEP.

Carry on, I'm with you.

THAT'S AS FAR AS I'VE GOT.

You're making up a story.

I THOUGHT I'D GIVE IT A TRY.

This Nnvsnu the Tsrungh – there's a lot of you in him, isn't there?

WELL, YOU KNOW HOW IT IS – THIS IS MY FIRST TIME.

That's all right, you're doing very well. There's nothing wrong with using yourself but you have to dress it up a bit, put in a little sex and violence, a little excitement. Not too much thinking in the ultimate deep.

NNVSNU THE TSRUNGH IS THINKING VIOLENTLY.

Of what?

OF GOING AFTER WHOEVER PULLED THE GREAT SNYUKH.

What was the Great Snyukh?

IT WAS THE BLUG OF NEXO VOLLMA.

The Blug of Nexo Vollma. I like that. I should think it was about forty feet high with a thousand tentacles and it left a slimy track.

NEXO VOLLMA IS THE BLUGHOLE OF THE UNIVERSE.

You mean plughole. Nexo Vollma is the plughole of the universe and the Great Snyukh was the plug. In that case the Great Snyukh must have been a good deal bigger than I thought.

130

IT WAS A WHOLE LOT BIGGER THAN ANY PLUG YOU CAN THINK OF, AND IT GOT PULLED. BUT IN THAT UNIMAGINABLE MOMENT BEFORE THE BIG WHOOSH, SNYUKH! INTO THE BLUGHOLE WENT NNVSNU THE TSRUNGH.

He saved us all.

HE DID WHAT HAD TO BE DONE BUT NOW HE THINKS VIOLENT THOUGHTS. FROM THE BLUGHOLE IN THE BLACKNESS OF THE HURGO MURMUS, FROM THE UTTERMOST DEPTHS OF THE ULTIMATE DEEP HE SENDS HIS MIND AFTER THOSE WHO PULLED THE GREAT SNYUKH, THE BLUG OF NEXO VOLLMA.

Who did it? Who pulled the Great Snyukh?

THE DEEPLY BAD ONES DID IT.

Why did they do it?

THEY WANTED TO HEAR THE BIG WHOOSH.

The bastards.

DEEPLY BAD.

But Nnvsnu the Tsrungh is sending his mind after them. How does he send his mind?

HE SENDS HIS MIND AS MEGAHERTZ, AS QUESTING SIGNAL FROM THE DISTANT DEEPS. AS THE SEEKER FROM NEXO VOLLMA IT SWEEPS ALL FREQUENCIES BUT HE CAN'T FIND THE DEEPLY BAD ONES.

He puts out a call on the emergency band, I said: DEEP MIND IN PURSUIT OF DEEPLY BAD ONES, REQUIRES ASSISTANCE.

BACK COMES THE MESSAGE, said the Kraken: ROGER, DEEP MIND, WILL ASSIST.

IDENTIFY YOURSELF, says Nnvsnu, I said.

I AM NABILCA, THING OF DARKNESS, IS THE RESPONSE, said the Kraken.

Nabilca, Thing of Darkness, I said, is really Wendy Nelson, a marine biologist. She was scuba diving when she lost consciousness and woke up in the secret undersea headquarters of the Nexo Foundation.

SWORN ENEMIES OF THE DEEPLY BAD ONES. THE NEXO FOUNDATION FIGHTS THE FORCES OF EVIL AND HAS DEDICATED ITSELF TO AVENGING THE EMBLUGMENT OF NNVSNU THE TSRUNGH. THEY IMPLANTED A RADIO IN WENDY NELSON'S HEAD SO SHE CAN COMMUNICATE WITH NNVSNU THE TSRUNGH.

Why don't they get Nnvsnu out of the blughole?

BECAUSE THE BLUGHOLE IS WHERE THE MOTHERCODE IS

131

TRANSMITTED FROM AND THE TRANSMISSION MUSTN'T STOP. THE GREAT SNYUKH USED TO DO IT BUT SINCE THE DEEPLY BAD ONES PULLED THE GREAT SNYUKH NNVSNU'S BEEN DOING IT.

The mothercode is what holds the universe together and of course the Deeply Bad Ones are after it.

IN THE BLACKNESS NNVSNU THE TSRUNGH TRANSMITS THE MOTHERCODE; SPINNING HIS MIND LIKE A PRAYER WHEEL HE REVOLVES CONTINUALLY THE NUMINOSITIES AND NEXIALITIES THAT COMMUNICATE THE UNIVERSE TO ITSELF.

What does Nnvsnu the Tsrungh actually look like?

ACTUALLY HE'S NOT PROPERLY A HE AND HE'S NOTHING YOU COULD PICTURE IN YOUR MIND. WHAT WE'RE TALKING ABOUT HERE IS A SPACE–TIME SINGULARITY WHICH IS IN FACT A NEURON OF THE COSMIC MIND TO WHICH THIS UNIVERSE HAS OCCURRED. SIMILARLY THE GREAT SNYUKH IS A SIMPLIFICATION OF A CUSP OF NEGATIVE PROBABILITY. ONCE INVERTED IT REVERSES ITS POLARITY AND BECOMES AN ACCELERATOR OF EVENT.

It might even be a TV series with a lot of special effects and some really top-class hardware. The Nexo Foundation has all kinds of displays and flashing lights and digital controls to monitor the shifting of probabilities as Nnvsnu the Tsrungh and Nabilca, Thing of Darkness who is really Wendy Nelson, fight the Deeply Bad Ones and various other forces of evil. Wendy Nelson's cover is marine biology but she's also a black belt in three or four martial arts, a top mathematician and physicist and an ace mechanic and driver. Sometimes in a violent action scene the bad guys will say, 'Get the girl!' and they'll grab her and take her to a hideout and tie her up but they never tear her clothes off or take advantage of her.

WHY DON'T THEY TEAR HER CLOTHES OFF AND TAKE ADVANTAGE OF HER?

For the same reason they can never shoot straight: they've got no self-confidence. That's why they're the bad guys – repeated failures have made them bitter and antisocial.

WELL, WHAT DO YOU THINK? CAN YOU DO ANYTHING WITH IT?

I'll have a go. First I'll try it as a comic, I'll work up a couple of episodes and show them to Bill Novad at Novad Ventures, they do Captain Pituitary.

GOOD LUCK.

Thank you, and thanks for your help.

22 Questions

The morning after my talk with the Kraken I was ready to begin work on *The Seeker from Nexo Vollma*. As one will at such times, I found myself taking stock of the present situation and reviewing recent events. What about the head of Orpheus, was I ever going to see it again? I supposed not, probably the angina had signalled my being dropped from its thoughts back into ordinary life. Where was it now? Had it gone back for another go with Fallok? Had it found someone new?

23   I Mention This

Often in my researches I've come across old books of a specialist nature in which the author, usually a retired wing-commander, expresses in a modest foreword the hope that the little volume may be a *vade mecum* for the model steam engineer, coarse angler, sado-masochist or whatever. I feel that way about these pages: I hope that this little volume may be a *vade mecum* not so much for the specialist as for others like me – the general struggler and straggler, the person for whom the whole sweep of consciousness is often too much. Here I am reminded of the words of H. P. Lovecraft:

> The most merciful thing in the world, I think, is the inability of the human mind to correlate all its contents.

Persons for whom the whole sweep of consciousness is often too much are prone, when in a weakened condition, to wear themselves out by looking feverishly for things they cannot find. I've described my desk and I might as well say right here that my whole workroom is in pretty much the same state of terminal clutter. Oh yes, I have filing cabinets and folders to put things in but life isn't that simple and there are always papers that hide themselves in odd places or in wrong folders.

I mention this because no sooner had I typed the title *The Seeker from Nexo Vollma* on to the screen than I found myself trying to remember where I'd put a loose folder containing a several years' old article from *Newsweek* on mud-brick architecture. I had no need of that information at the time but my mind in its irregular and desultory patrolling of its boundaries had happened to note that it didn't know at that moment where the mud-brick architecture article was. So I went looking for it, at first casually and then seriously and with hot waves of aggravation flooding over me like colour changes on a cuttlefish.

I found the folder after about five hours, it was stuck between two books on Çatal Hüyük. By then it was time for lunch. After lunch I had a kip then read over what I'd typed out during my conversation with the Kraken the day before. Good God, what rubbish it seemed. By then it was drink time which made the burden of my critical faculty easier to bear.

The main thing to keep in mind in the situation I have just described is that nothing is gained by pretending not to care about the mud-brick article; on the contrary, any lapse in concentration may well result in falling off a ladder or stepping into a month-old mug of coffee. The search for the mud-brick article must simply be accepted as that part of the work that precedes reading what one has written yesterday and recognizing it as rubbish.

24   Not Rubbish

Nnvsnu the Tsrungh stayed with me, however. Poor bastard, I thought, stuck down there in the blughole of the universe, ceaselessly spinning his mind like a prayer wheel as he transmitted the mothercode. Late that night as I thought about it I realized that he himself was ignorant of that mothercode; he span his mind because the pressures of the ultimate deep forced him to do so, and through the centrifuge of his consciousness flung out, unknown to him, the numinosities and nexialities that were the frail but constant web of the universe.

Nabilca, his thing of darkness, his sender and receiver of messages to and from the deep, would he ever see her, would he ever touch her?

Not likely.

25 Longer than the Moment

So *The Seeker from Nexo Vollma* wasn't rubbish and I was going to have a go with it. The next morning I was at my desk early and keen to begin.

It's funny, though, how the odd detail will stick in the mind and give you no peace. I found myself remembering the morning when Melanie and I had first met at Hermes Sound-ways; she'd left a tape cassette with Istvan Fallok. I'd always wondered what was on that cassette. It was certainly none of my business but it was just one of those little things that I wanted to know about.

So I rang her up at home. No answer. Just then the post arrived and I went to get it. Among the bills and letters was a little padded brown envelope with a cassette inside. On the cassette was written:

Herman, this is from me.

M

I knew what it was before I played it but I played it anyhow.

'Herman,' said her voice, 'I don't want this to be just words on a piece of paper but I'm too much of a coward to look you in the eye and say what I'm going to say and the telephone is no good either.'

Hearing her voice like that without seeing her there in front of me I found her oddly more real to me than she had been. This was Melanie who was a mystery to me and, as everyone is, to herself, whose thoughts I didn't know, whose being had its own spacetime and its own world line separate from mine. We had talked intimately, had been lovers briefly, yet her voice came to me as strange and distant as those many voices from far away reflected from the ionosphere and expressed digitally on my radio's frequency counter.

'Death is longer than life,' she said, 'and the death of each moment is longer than the moment. The goneness is what we're left with, maybe some of us more than others. It's very hard to *have* anything, isn't it? Like our blue-black shining rainy night, when I call it to mind it's the going-awayness of it, the goneness of it that I taste. I've always been a sort of phoney percy, you see – Persephone more than Eurydice, with my own little dark realm. Or I'm like Rilke's Eurydike, so full of my large death that I understand nothing. I suppose that's why I need, how shall I put it, more of a red-pyjama type than you are. I lied to you about General Sphincter's mistress, I was with Sol that weekend and I was with him the other night when you rang up at three o'clock in the morning to tell him you wouldn't do the Orpheus thing for *Classique*. So at least you don't have to feel guilty about me, I did it to you before you did it to me. Goodbye, Herman. We'll undoubtedly see each other here and there in the normal course of things and I don't expect it'll be awkward. I have a feeling that now you'll be able to write again, better than before. And it was nice, that blue-black shining rainy night, it really was.'

26   Roughage

'I like the texture of it, Herman,' said Bill Novad. 'It's got the right polypeptides if you know what I mean.'

'Amino acids?'

'That's it: primordial soup and all that. All your really deep comics have it, and if you can't be deep you'll never make it in comics. Nnvsnu the Tsrungh gets to me.'

'I was hoping it would.'

'How do you feel about the backs of cereal boxes?'

'As noumenon or phenomenon?'

'As an art form.'

'They seem to have fallen into disuse; I remember when they had little stories on them.'

'Right. They've gone with our pre-atom-bomb innocence. We're living in a time that cries out for the reaffirmation of traditional values. Used properly the back of a cereal box is to literature what Buddy Holly is to music: it's got drive, it's got soul, it's got bebop. Look at this.' He took a box of Holywell Corn Flakes out of a desk drawer and showed me first the front and then the back of it. They were both the same, with a picture of a bowl of corn flakes and the words CORN FLAKES. 'Do you believe that?' he said. 'Two fronts, no back, you don't know where you are with it, your whole day starts off funny. Put a comic on one side and that's the back, you eat your corn flakes and you read it, you know where you are.' He tapped one of the two fronts. 'Can you see it right there, THE SEEKER FROM NEXO VOLLMA?' He said it in capital letters.

'I can see it,' I said. I could too: the deeps were a strong purply-blue shading off to black. Nnvsnu the Tsrungh, obscure and amorphous, was a dim blue-green. I could see myself reading it at breakfast, could feel the peace and natural order of it. BONGGGGG, rang the great bell of the deep as Nabilca, responsive to the call of Nnvsnu, plunged down, down, down through green and sunlit waters.

'And you *will* see it,' he said. 'Slithe & Tovey have just given me the Holywell breakfast line to do: that's corn flakes, bran flakes, and muesli. I think bran is what we want for *The Seeker*.'

'It's more regular.'

'It's your *Guardian*-reader market. Do a good job on this and you can have the corn flakes as well.'

'What about the muesli?'

'No comics on the muesli, just recipes. Can you give me six episodes in a fortnight and six more two weeks later?'

'What kind of money are we talking about?'

'Five hundred up front for development, one hundred per episode. Flat fee, no royalties.'

'Seventeen hundred isn't much for what they're getting.'

'It is when you think of how many guys are trying to break into cereal boxes. Plus you'll probably do the whole twelve in two nights or maybe even one night. Once you've got your original premise it's a piece of cake.'

'More like a load of bran. Holywell can have first cereal rights but the characters belong to me and if I do a book or a TV series or a line of toys they've got no part of it.'

'You should be so lucky. I'll talk to Slithe & Tovey and see what kind of a deal we can do and get back to you later. OK?'

The deeps were gone, the hiss and rush of traffic overran the moving of great waters and the darkness. I was standing by the bicycle shop that was under the offices of Novad Ventures in Gray's Inn Road. It was like coming out of the cinema, I was blinking in the sunlight. The terror and the excitement slid back behind the screen of everyday and I walked slowly to the underground.

27   To Borrow the World

I'd no plans to go anywhere but home but when OXFORD CIRCUS appeared in the train windows I got out and walked over to Hermes Soundways.

Fallok was sitting in his electronic twilight holding a small terrestrial globe, a cheap tin one, badly dented, with no base. Through the closed door I could hear the Hermes music.

'I never should have let him do it,' he said as I came in.

'Let whom do what?'

'I never should have let Kraken get his head zapped.'

'Kraken! Do you mean to tell me that Mr Deep Mind himself came to you with art trouble?'

'How can you joke about it with the poor bastard dead?'

'Dead! Of what?'

'Heart attack. I think he may have had some trouble with the head of Orpheus.'

'What happened?'

'After our lunch at L'Escargot I was walking slowly back here when I heard a voice speaking to me from a dustbin in Wardour Street and it was the head. I didn't want to stand there in the street talking to it so I wrapped it up in the *Guardian* and brought it here. I was surprised to see it on the loose and I rang you up but there was no answer.'

'I must've been in hospital by then.'

'Anything bad?'

'Bit of angina. What happened with the head?'

'I asked it what it wanted and it wouldn't answer but it began to sing. I was recording the singing when Kraken dropped in and asked me why I had a microphone in front of a perfectly silent tin globe. So I told him about it and then he wanted to get his head done so he could see the head of Orpheus too. We had a session but he didn't see the head and he asked if he could borrow the globe; I gave it to him and he left. He'd said he'd ring me up to let me know how he was getting on but after three or four days I heard from Hilary

Forthryte that he was dead. He was found sitting in a chair with the globe in his lap.

'Poor Kraken. I doubt that he and the head would have got on very well.'

'Actually he was a pretty boring guy,' said Fallok, 'but I liked his films.'

28 No More *Klage*

It was the fourth of December and the *Geburtstag* of Rainer Maria Rilke, said the girl from Tirana, and she went on to read 'Orpheus, Eurydike, Hermes'. I'm always forgetting what I read, so the same lines can be new to me many times, as now when I heard her enchanting voice say:

> *daß eine Welt aus Klage ward, in der*
> that a world became out of lament, in which

> *alles noch einmal da war: Wald und Tal*
> everything existed once more: forest and valley

> *und Weg und Ortschaft, Feld und Fluß und Tier;*
> and path and hamlet, field and river and animal;

> *und daß um diese Klage-Welt, ganz so*
> and that around this lament-world, just as

> *wie um die andre Erde, eine Sonne*
> around the other earth, a sun

> *und ein gestirnter stiller Himmel ging,*
> and a starry quiet sky went,

> *ein Klage-Himmel mit entstellten Sternen – :*
> a lament-sky with disfigured stars – :

As once before, the words departed and I heard only that sweet and promising voice of Eurydice unfound and unlost.

'Right,' I said, 'no more *Klage*,' and when I looked up at the Vermeer girl it was Medusa I saw, flickering and friendly, trusting me with the idea of her.